THE MURDER OF AN ANGEL

JAMES PATTERSON is one of the best-known and biggest-selling writers of all time. His books have sold in excess of 325 million copies worldwide and he has been the most borrowed author in UK libraries for the past nine years in a row. He is the author of some of the most popular series of the past two decades – the Alex Cross, Women's Murder Club, Detective Michael Bennett and Private novels – and he has written many other number one bestsellers including romance novels and stand-alone thrillers.

James is passionate about encouraging children to read. Inspired by his own son who was a reluctant reader, he also writes a range of books for young readers including the Middle School, I Funny, Treasure Hunters, House of Robots, Confessions and Maximum Ride series. James is the proud sponsor of the World Book Day Award and has donated millions in grants to independent bookshops. He lives in Florida with his wife and son.

CONFESSIONS
THE MURDER OF AN ANGEL

JAMES PATTERSON
AND MAXINE PAETRO

Young Arrow is part of the Penguin Random House
group of companies whose addresses can be found at
global.penguinrandomhouse.com

Penguin
Random House
UK

Copyright © James Patterson 2015
Excerpt from *First Love* copyright © 2014 by James Patterson
Excerpt from *First Love* photos by Sasha Illingworth

James Patterson has asserted his right to be identified as the
author of this Work in accordance with the Copyright,
Designs and Patents Act 1988.

First published by Young Arrow in 2015
First published in paperback by Young Arrow in 2016

www.penguin.co.uk

A CIP catalogue record for this book
is available from the British Library.

ISBN 9781784750213

Printed and bound in Great Britain by Clays Ltd, St Ives Plc

MIX
Paper from
responsible sources
FSC
www.fsc.org   FSC® C018179

Penguin Random House is committed to a sustainable
future for our business, our readers and our planet.
This book is made from Forest Stewardship Council®
certified paper.

1

THE SO-CALLED REAL WORLD

1

Hello, friend.

I have a lot to tell you...good and bad.

Today was *huge*.

It's been three months since I checked myself into Waterside, an exclusive rehab facility for those who are psychologically on the edge—or *were*, like me. By the time I got dressed this morning, my discharge papers were already signed and I was more or less ready to leave the loony bin and reenter the "real world."

It was early yet, about eight fifteen on a cold winter morning. I was relaxing on a fancy teak bench outside Waterside's grand pillared entrance overlooking the Hudson River in northern Manhattan, waiting for my three brothers and uncle to pick me up. I had dressed appropriately in all black: a Hervé Léger hooded coat, a turtleneck sweater, stretch wool pants, and flat-heeled Louboutin boots. I even wore lipstick and a silver headband in my dark hair, which had grown almost to my jawline in the three months since the three-alarm fire, the fatal car crash, and the total destruction of my innocence. More on that later.

My therapist, Dr. Robosson, had told me after our final morning session, "You sound very good, Tandy. Once you're back in school and settled in your new home, the routines of your New York life will reassert themselves and you'll be better than ever. Let's set up an outpatient schedule soon. I'm here for you, always."

She walked me outside and gave me a pillowy, perfumed hug, a kiss on the cheek, and a card with her cell phone number. My eyes got teary, but I was glad to say good-bye to this place.

When I had first checked myself into Waterside, Dr. Robosson had said to me, "Tandy, you've lived through fire and rain, and weathered more storms in the last year than most people have even heard about in their entire lives. If all that's happened hadn't devastated you, I'd really worry. You've been badly hurt, even if the scars don't show. You just need to talk and heal. Get a good amount of the three Rs: rest, relaxation, and reality check. Am I right?"

She had been indisputably right.

My parents were dead. I'd been accused of killing them, viciously attacked by the press, and even jailed. I'd beaten back the forces of bad, worse, and criminally heinous. I'd solved crimes: my parents' deaths to start with, and then the murders of friends and strangers. All while uncovering mysteries, long-held secrets, and epic lives of blood relatives that surely had a profound and sometimes damaging impact on mine.

Before the events of this year, I had been known as a brainiac, a nerd with a gift for sharp analysis and first-class problem solving. I was completely unemotional, and therefore absolutely clearheaded. Those are the skills that made me a natural detective.

But by the time I turned myself over to the professional care of Waterside's psychiatric staff, I had changed. I felt everything. I cared too much. I was sleepless, jumpy, emotionally ravaged: a ragged tangle of nerves.

Now, after the intense psychotherapeutic intervention that included marathon talk therapy, meditation, steam baths, comfort foods, and dreamless sleep, I had metamorphosed from a traumatized teenager who'd been repeatedly subjected to mortal danger and shocking betrayal into a traumatized teenager who finally understood the truth.

And what was the truth? The truth was that I'd been deceived by so many people I loved, I no longer trusted *anyone*. It wasn't my fault. I'd been naïve. Accordingly, I'd been crushed but not broken. I was still emotional, but the Sullivanians, Freudians, Jungians, Skinnerians, and Far Eastern disciples among the Waterside staff all agreed. I wasn't insane.

I was *mad*.

Madder than hell.

2

My anger was real and justified. But would anger cure me...or destroy me?

That was the question.

The longer I sat on the bench in front of Waterside, staring at the river and the droning highway below, the more agitated I became.

I already regretted tearing myself from my lounge chair in the quiet, fern-filled solarium where my to-do list never had more than two items: Sip tea and listen to good music.

Instead, I was dressed for my first day of school, and despite assurances from the shrinks, my sudden flashes of anger troubled me. I wondered if I was really ready to take on the outside world, which could be crazier than I ever was.

My uncle Jacob had wanted me to check out of Waterside last week and come home to our new apartment for a few days so that I could get my bearings before starting school.

But I hadn't been ready to leave the warm embrace of Waterside, the spa days, the luxury of being treated like a fragile baby chick.

I had put off leaving until the last minute—which was now. I was rubbing my arms against the cold breeze coming off the river when I heard the crunch of tires on gravel and turned to see a long black limo with tinted glass pulling into the semicircular driveway.

A driver got out of the car. He was six feet tall, muscle-bound in black livery. He wore a black driver's hat and had tattoos on his knuckles.

He said, "Ms. Angel? I'm Leo Peavey. I work for your family."

Unsmiling, he picked up my backpack and opened the back door for me. I looked inside, expecting to see my brothers and my uncle Jacob, but only Hugo, my youngest bro, an eleven-year-old master of troublemaking, was there.

"Where is everyone?" I said to Hugo.

"*I'm* here. Sorry to disappoint."

I opened my arms to the little monster who had been coming to visit me just about every week since my admission to Waterside.

He spoke with his face pressed into my coat. "Have fun at Waterside Penitentiary?"

"Of course," I said, kissing his head. "It was like Christmas and the Cherry Blossom Festival all rolled into one."

"Ha. What did they do to you, Tandy?"

"They forced me to sleep late, drink peppermint tea, read *Harry Potter*, and listen to Chopin. All at the same time."

"Sounds horrible," Hugo said. He meant it.

I cracked up.

My little bro went on. "Uncle Jake and Matty are setting up your computer. Harry had early practice this morning. I hope we get there in time."

Getting there in time meant arriving at school before the window for enrollment in the second term closed. I couldn't miss that.

Leo had just negotiated the curving on-ramp to the Henry Hudson when, without warning, our wheels failed to grip the slippery highway and we went into a long, slow sideways skid on the ice. I gripped Hugo's hand as we slewed across the lanes. And then I saw a dark SUV behind us, bearing down on us at high speed as we spun around.

Time slowed, and I saw exactly how our car would get T-boned at sixty miles an hour. I was already hearing our screams and the ripping, screeching sound of metal on metal.

I remembered how a black Escalade chased my car not too long ago...and how that pursuit ended in many horrifying deaths.

I grabbed Hugo and braced for the crash.

The last thing I saw was the SUV—windshield tinted impenetrably black—before squeezing my eyes shut, waiting for the inevitable.

3

Car horns began to blare.

I opened my eyes. Just in time to see the SUV shooting past our still-spinning car, skimming a guardrail, then getting traction and speeding off.

Our driver wrenched back control of the limo, and his eyes shot to the rearview mirror as he shouted, "You kids all right?"

Hugo was as pale as milk, and my heart was still flailing in terror. I exhaled shakily and said, "We're good," but the shock of the narrowly missed accident wouldn't fade.

I was lucky to be alive.

As the limo sped along the highway, I tried to put the

accident out of my mind for my sake and Hugo's, and ready myself for the looming reality of high school.

I had always been regarded by my peers as odd, weird, and, at the very least, a peculiar girl. But as odd, weird, and peculiar as I was, my three brothers belonged in the square-peg-round-hole category just as much as me.

There was a reason for this.

I thought back on my session with Dr. Robosson less than an hour ago. We were sitting in her office, wrapping up before my departure from Waterside.

She said, "Tandy, I know how you feel about medication, but I've written you a prescription for a mild tranquilizer. You can take one in the morning before school, and one before bed, if you feel too agitated to sleep. They're very safe."

She tore the prescription from the pad, but I was already shaking my head *No, no, no.*

"No more pills, Dr. Robosson. I'm done with them, forever."

I was remembering other pills that had brought me and my siblings to this place and time.

Our overachieving parents, Maud and Malcolm Angel, had set impossibly high standards of performance for us. And to help us reach those standards, we were all given a daily regimen of pills produced by the family business, Angel Pharmaceuticals.

We were told the pretty, colorful pills were vitamins. In fact, they were drugs designed to boost certain talents many times over while completely repressing our emotions—which Malcolm and Maud believed are detrimental to success.

Because of the pills, Hugo has the strength of an adult male athlete. Our older brother, Matthew, is a Heisman Trophy–winning football player for the New York Giants.

Their nuclear tempers are also legendary. When Matty or Hugo gets mad, *run*. Run fast.

My twin brother, Harry, is an artistic and musical genius, but withdrawn and socially inept. I'm also very awkward around people, but like my father, I have a highly scientific mind. I have the ability to look at disparate parts and intuit what the whole will look like. I'm nearly always right.

But until last year when I stopped taking the pills, I had no feelings, no messy emotions, and, like Matty, had been called a sociopath more than once. I had the perfect personality for a corporate CEO, and my parents hoped I would head up the family business one day.

Even then, I thought I'd rather be dead.

The full truth about how the pills changed the regular-smart Angel kids into high-achieving, sociophobic *freaks* didn't come out until after our parents were gone. But charts of our progress, memos about the experiments, and the pills themselves remained.

The evidence was undeniable.

Maud, Malcolm, and our uncle Peter had willfully experimented on us and on other human lab animals before we were born. Some of those people—a lot of them just *kids*—had died.

And still, to this day, Angel Pharmaceuticals produces "the pills." Because they are called vitamins, they are not under the purview of the FDA. Our despicable uncle Peter, currently the sole proprietor of the company, is cagey enough not to sell the pills in the United States. Instead, he ships them overseas.

I've grown up fast in the last few months, and I'm still working things out. I don't yet know how, but I'm sure of at least this much: As soon as possible, I'm going to bring Angel Pharmaceuticals down—board up the headquarters, sue the hell out of my uncle Peter, and burn the factory to the ground.

CONFESSION

I hated my parents.

But I loved them, too.

Malcolm and Maud were ruthless, never allowing me or my brothers to accept failure or even second best. When we did excel, it was always expected and rarely celebrated. Punishments were severe, involving anything from copying whole books—in perfect calligraphy—to military boot camps. Displays of emotion were strictly forbidden.

Can you imagine being a little kid in that kind of environment? No wonder we all turned out so...peculiar.

But then, there were the other times. I remember snuggling between them in their enormous bed, being read to from gorgeous picture books in Urdu or Japanese. Playing dress-up in

Maud's closet, tripping in her stilettos and dragging her furs around the room like a Hollywood star. Watching Malcolm experimenting with a new recipe in the kitchen, taste-testing his always delicious gourmet dishes.

When I found out about the pills and how our parents used us as their personal guinea pigs, I was enraged—but not really surprised.

After all, if the drugs were able to turn people into superhuman genius prodigies, Malcolm and Maud were going to make sure that their children would be *first in line* to take them.

Side effects be damned.

4

I watched the highway roll past the car windows. Twenty minutes after leaving Waterside, Leo slowed to approach the old spired church with stained-glass windows on the corner of Seventy-Seventh and Columbus.

This church had been repurposed as All Saints Academy, and during the school year, it was like an old-fashioned one-room schoolhouse where students of all grades took their classes together. But far from having lessons in a rickety building on the prairie, we were tutored under the vaulted ceiling of a Gothic cathedral on a beautiful New York City avenue.

Up ahead, I saw a dozen kids I knew sitting together

on the wide church steps, kidding one another and laughing.

"We made it," Hugo said to me. "We beat the bell."

Before the car had fully stopped, Hugo bolted out right into traffic. I yelled and Leo braked hard. He ejected himself from the driver's seat, and with horns blowing behind us, he ran around the nose of the limo, grabbed Hugo by the arm, and hoisted him onto the sidewalk.

"You want to get killed, Mr. Hugo? Why? You're the boy with everything."

As I got out on the sidewalk, Leo handed me my book bag—a python Proenza Schouler satchel—and his card, saying, "If you need me, just call."

Then Leo Peavey sped off and disappeared into the morning rush hour traffic.

Standing in front of All Saints, my school since kindergarten, I had a flash of first-day-of-school excitement. I wished Harry was here with me, but he was off at an intensive music workshop that got him permission to be out of All Saints this first week.

Then I heard a familiar voice calling, "Hey, crazy."

I turned and saw C.P.—my former best friend and current worst nightmare—with her hands on her hips and a nasty grin on her face, showing she wasn't kidding. She was taunting me for real.

Memories of the last time I'd seen C.P. hit me with the force of a tsunami. On that unthinkable day, the traitor had been standing in her lacy lingerie, clinging possessively to James, the boy I had loved with my whole heart.

Of course, that meant that he'd betrayed me, too.

5

When I met Claudia Portman, aka C.P., she was an out-
cast, like me. She could be bitchy or funny, depending on
how you took it. She had her own witchy fashion style,
which she mostly pulled off. After her former friends
abandoned her for behavior unbefitting a bestie, she and
I quickly joined forces as a bonded pair of inseparable
oddballs.

But last year, C.P. had deceived me unforgivably by
hooking up with James. Even though she apologized way
after the fact, saying, "I just couldn't help myself, Tandy,"
her matter-of-fact apology was so transparently false, I
could never trust her again.

There were three sides to this story: hers, his, and mine. But who cares about theirs? My side had been vetted and psychiatrically approved. I was doubly wronged by any standard, and I didn't have the time or grace within me to forgive or forget either one of them.

I understand that if you can't forgive, anger takes over you. And I say, "Bring it on." Remembering pain is how you learn never to let the cause of it happen again.

Now, standing in front of the school, with her taunt still hanging in the air, I faced C.P. head-on.

She looked different now.

She had extensions, good ones that made a cascade of honeyed brunette waves down to her shoulders. She was wearing a tiny Nicole Miller skirt and a tight top with sheer netting from shoulder to shoulder, something I would never dare to wear to school. This was the high-priced-hooker look favored by private school girls, but it really begged the question of who here was the crazy one.

Her insult hung between us like a freeze-frame of a tennis serve. Then the action resumed.

"So the nutcase returns," she said. "Did you escape? Hey, everyone, the House of Psychosis is missing a lunatic."

I took aim at my former friend, shouting, "I could vomit up alphabet soup and make more sense than you."

She said, "Really? I'm right here, psycho. Dazzle me with your wit. If they didn't electroshock it out of you, that is."

With that, Hugo jumped between the two of us, pointed his phone at C.P., and snapped a picture. He examined it and said, "C.P., you ugly."

"Shut up, you little tapeworm," she snarled. Then other voices cut in with more insults, calling me a lunatic, a nutjob, batshit crazy.

C.P. was taunting me again: "Are those your *dead mother*'s clothes, Tandy? I just *love* the boots."

Instead of walking past her, or laughing in her face, I shot back, "I got them in Paris. Where'd you get *your* outfit, C.P.? Sluts R Us?"

"Oh, too funny, Tandoori. Look, why don't you just go back to Water-Fried until you're normal? Which will be . . . oh, exactly *never*."

I was gathering myself for a sharp comeback when Hugo stepped up to C.P., pulled back his arm, and, before I even had a chance to freak, punched her right in the gut.

This was no joke. Thanks to the pills, Hugo was *strong*. I saw C.P.'s feet lift off the ground as she fell backward onto the sidewalk and let out a stunned grunt.

Another girl sputtered at Hugo, "You *psycho*. You can't hit girls!"

Hugo said, "What *girl*? All I see is a pathetic bitch who asked for what I gave her. Actually, she demanded it."

A whistle blew sharply, and we all turned to see a florid man with flyaway hair and a small mouth that was pinched around a whistle. His little black eyes were like bullets behind his glasses.

He shouted, "Everyone freeze!"

Friend, all this happened within the first ten minutes of my return to All Saints Academy.

6

Our former headmaster, Mr. Thibodaux, had been a tough disciplinarian, but very caring. It seems that he had left during my absence from All Saints, and his replacement was barring our path to the school.

He introduced himself haughtily. "I'm Dr. Felix Oppenheimer. Who are you?"

"That's Tandoori Angel," said one of C.P.'s posse before I could respond.

"Hugo's sister? I should have guessed."

C.P. was on her feet by then, her eyes watering with either pain or humiliation, but she was standing—which meant that Hugo had held back with his punch. Thank God. He could have killed her.

"Are you all right?" the headmaster asked C.P.

"He *hit* me," she said, pointing to Hugo, "really hard. Christ, I might not be able to have babies because of him."

"Claudia, skip the blasphemy and go see the nurse," said the headmaster. "You two," he said, pointing at Hugo and me. "Stay right here. Everyone else, go inside—*now*."

He got on his phone and made a couple of phone calls with his back to us. Then he waited on the sidewalk until Leo reappeared with the car.

Our driver was still applying the brakes when Dr. Oppenheimer delivered both a threat and the biggest insult of all.

"Hugo, the next time you use physical violence, I'll call the police. Effective tomorrow, you will write a letter of apology to Ms. Portman and you will read it out loud in assembly or you will not be allowed to attend All Saints this term. I've been in touch with your guardian.

"Tandoori, because of this ruckus, you've missed your deadline for admission. I'm sorry for you. But you didn't plan appropriately. Right now, both of you must leave."

Hugo sputtered. He was about to launch a retort, but I put my hand on his shoulder and told Dr. Oppenheimer we were both sorry for our behavior.

Hugo wriggled under my hand, but he didn't say a word.

When my brother and I were in the car, the registrar, Mrs. Benardete, bent to the car window and said to me, "You can fill out the registration form online, Tandy. I'll work on the headmaster, but you must send me the paperwork today."

I nodded, then sank so low into the backseat that I was practically lying down. Hugo threw his arms around me and started crying. Despite his strength, he was still just a little kid, and I was the only mom he had. I patted his back and said, "It's okay. Don't cry." But I was scared for him.

I hadn't started this fight with C.P. I hadn't started *any* of the fights with C.P. But if there had been any question in my mind before, there was none now.

This was *war*.

7

The car was silent, a swift projectile, impervious to outside forces, and Leo was taking us "home" to a place that didn't feel like it yet.

Let me explain.

After my mother's hedge fund went bust, she was sued into the next century. She owed fifty million dollars to creditors, which was more than we had or could borrow.

The bankruptcy of Leading Hedge forced the sale of our incredible co-op in the legendary Dakota apartment building. But days before we were to be turned out on the street, Uncle Jacob took me and my brothers to Paris.

This voyage and our time in Paris was a lifeline of the most magnificent kind. Our uncle, whom we had only known for a short time, had pulled some very old strings, and we learned that we were heirs to a large inheritance. Our benefactor was Hilda Angel, our father's glamorous mother, who had died before any of her grandchildren had been born.

But she had planned for us.

Gram Hilda's bequests had conditions and a team of stuffy legal advisors attached. But for the present, her estate paid each of us a generous monthly allowance and bought us a new home in the San Remo Apartments.

The San Remo is a grande dame of an apartment building that was built in 1930. Like the Dakota, the building takes up an entire block on Central Park West. One of the San Remo's unique features is that above the eighteenth floor, the building is topped by two ten-story towers.

We were closing in on Seventy-Fifth Street when Hugo sat up and said, "See that, Tandy? Our apartment, way up on the sixteenth and seventeenth floors, just under the north tower—guess how long it takes for an orange juice balloon to hit the sidewalk from way up there."

"Hugo!"

"Kidding. Just *kidding*."

A few minutes later, Leo cruised up to the curb and braked the car outside the stupendous building.

I drifted through the doorman-flanked entrance behind

Hugo, passed the elegant common rooms, and stepped into an elevator. After a long upward whoosh, the doors opened inside the only apartment on the sixteenth floor— a duplex, and it was ours.

Uncle Jacob was standing in the foyer, waiting. The look on his face showed a colorful range of feelings: relief, dismay, and pure cold anger.

"Oppenheimer called," he said. "How could all this happen before the bell? I'm getting flashbacks to all the other beyond unpleasant phone calls I've had to field because of you children."

I said under my breath, "We'll always have Paris."

"What was that, Tandy?"

I never got a chance to answer.

8

Uncle Jacob, my father's oldest brother, is a former Israeli commando. He may be old—approaching fifty—but he's a proven killer. And he'd sacrificed his good life in Israel to be our guardian.

He had saved my life several times in the first three months that he lived with us—one of the many ways he'd shown that he loved us.

But Uncle Jake was no pushover. Hugo was about to run past him, but Jacob put out his arm and stopped him cold.

"Hugo. What is this crap?" he asked as I floated past them, taking in the sights of our childhood, wide-eyed with appreciation for the artifacts we were able to salvage and trying to move beyond their argument.

Hanging in the foyer was the UFO chandelier from my childhood. Wired to the doorbell, it was a silver saucer-shaped disc with lights that blinked in time to the theme song from the movie *Close Encounters of the Third Kind*, which it played when the bell rang.

Beyond the foyer was an unbelievably spacious living room with a marble fireplace, casement windows on three sides, and a terrace with a panoramic view of Central Park.

Inside the living room was the eccentric collection of hyperrealistic objets d'art my mother had loved to collect: Robert, the lifelike sculpture of a man drinking beer while watching TV in a recliner; Pegasus, a winged, white-lacquered piano that was Harry's own instrument, on which he practiced and played; and Mercurio, a merman hanging by his tail from the second-floor ceiling within the coil of the spiral staircase. Even the lipstick-red leather sofa and the Pork Chair, which had pig's feet and snorted when sat upon, were here.

I teared up for the second time today.

I knew that our attorney, Philippe Montaigne, had bought back these items when we came into our inheritance, but I hadn't seen them in so long, it was as if old deceased relatives had come back from the dead.

As I gawked, Jacob was having strong words with Hugo.

"Do you understand that you could be charged with assault, Hugo?"

"A misdemeanor," said Hugo. "Plus, I'm a minor."

Jacob went on. "If you've hurt C.P., you could be tried in juvenile court. Her parents have vast resources, and you, Hugo, are part of a family with what are called deep pockets. I hope I don't need to explain again that you could lose your inheritance."

Uncle Jake was referring to Gram Hilda's main condition for our inheritance, that we would lose it all if we "disgraced the family name."

"C.P. was verbally abusing Tandy," Hugo shot back.

Jacob said, "Violence is the last resort of cowards."

Hugo looked up at him, mouth opened. "But you're a soldier!"

The corners of Jacob's mouth turned up for a second. "Good job standing up for your sister," he said. "But no more violence, agreed?" Our uncle stretched out his hand.

Hugo grinned and shook hands with Jacob.

Which, when Hugo was involved, was not a promise of anything.

9

Jacob put his arm around my shoulders and walked with me into the living room. He was looking at my face, but his sleeves were rolled up and I was looking at his scarred forearms, a permanent reminder of the black night when he carried me out of Gram Hilda's burning house. My uncle Hero.

"Are you okay?"

"Never better," I chirped.

It was our private joke, and he laughed. It was a good laugh, hearty and masculine. I loved him. On the other hand—and there was always another hand—six months ago, I'd never heard of him. It was our loathsome uncle

Peter who had introduced my sibs and me to Jacob and turned over our guardianship to him.

"The rest of the day is all about you," Jacob said. "After that, it's back to swimming with the sharks."

"Fantastic," I said. "I can swim with the best of them."

"Quite true," he said. "Take a look at your room while Hugo and I go out for groceries. Here's your elevator key." He pulled it from the pocket of his khakis. "But stay here. Get to know your new phone. Change your passwords. Read a book. There are sandwich ingredients in the fridge."

I hugged my uncle, and when he said, "That way," I headed to the spiral staircase. We'd had just such a staircase in our old apartment. I whispered hey to Mercurio as I passed him, and when I got to the landing, I saw four open doors. Jacob's bedroom, Hugo's, Harry's, and the fourth was painted my color, firmament blue. That room was mine.

I clapped my hands over my mouth, walked through the doorway, and just stood there, taking in the open sky through the windows, the four-poster bed, the desk with a laptop in the center, and the bookshelves all around, holding my books and my specimens of branched coral.

On a dress form in the corner was my mother's jacket, the one Madonna had worn in the movie *Desperately*

Seeking Susan. It was a metallic greenish color with embroidery on the back, showing a pyramid with an eye on top, like the artwork on a dollar bill. I loved that jacket. It reminded me of the rarely seen, fun-loving parts of my mom's personality.

I went to the desk and opened my laptop. The software said, "Hi, Tandy."

Without even thinking, I opened my in-box, which was stuffed with hundreds of e-mails. I'm not going to lie to you, friend. I skimmed the list, my heart beating hard in my throat, looking for a message from James.

Partially relieved, but freshly disappointed, I found nothing that would jar my heart or wrack me with waves of pain and fury. I deleted huge blocks of out-of-date newsletters, sales pitches, and spam. And when I was done, I changed my password and installed the new encryption program Jacob had left for me.

After that, I uploaded Harry's music playlist and checked out my new iPhone and iPad.

When I heard the UFO toot its announcement that someone was at the door, I ran downstairs to greet my family. After some happy screams and dancing around on the beautiful parquet floors, dinner preparation commenced.

Harry and I had some quiet time as we figured out how to make crepes without a crepe pan.

He said to me, "You feeling okay?"

"Meaning?"

"Have you had a chance to process, uh, everything that's happened?"

"Everything? Sure, but I wouldn't say I'm cured."

An hour later, my older brother, Matty, arrived with his dreads tied back with a cord, his laser-blue eyes sparkling, and wearing his own New York Giants jersey under his jacket.

He held out a huge bunch of paper-wrapped roses. "Happy birthday, little sister," he said.

"It's not my birthday."

"Well, yeah, it is."

Crap. I'd forgotten my birthday. And Harry's!

10

"*I told you I could surprise her,*" Matty said to Uncle Jake. He tossed the roses down, picked me up, and twirled me around like I was five.

I laughed and beat his shoulders with little-girl fists. Finally, he put me back on my feet.

"Well, in my own defense," I said, resetting my hairband and smoothing my hair, "I haven't as much as seen a calendar in months. Or a clock, for that matter."

Everyone laughed at me, and Hugo said, "Welcome back to Planet Real Life, Tandy."

While I was being twirled and danced around and Harry came out of his room, Hugo had brought in a wooden crate marked SPECIAL DELIVERY, which he opened with a pry bar. Inside were wigs and masks, and we all grabbed for something outrageous. I'd always wanted to see what I looked like as a blonde—and from what I could see in the mirror over the sofa, I didn't look at all bad! And Jacob looked hilarious with a ponytail.

Over a very unusual dinner that included our favorite dishes from restaurants all over the city—tandoori prawns from the Indian restaurant on Columbus for me, smoked hot dogs from Hugo's favorite deli, and Szechuan alligator tail from Shun Lee West for Harry—we reminisced about other birthdays and I told tales about the real psych ward on the top floors of Waterside.

After dinner, we went back to the living room. Matty dragged Robert over to join us, saying, "No TV for a few minutes, okay, bro?"

Hugo took possession of the Pork Chair, and Harry and I sat on the floor and opened jokey presents: latex claws, big yellow teeth, and hot chili candy. Jacob brought in a chocolate cheesecake and set it down on the coffee table, and Harry and I blew out the seventeen candles together.

But the frosting on top was when my brilliant, talented, musical twin went to his Pegasus piano. He pushed up his sleeves, wiggled his fingers dramatically, and then sang a "Happy Birthday" song in a voice that reminded me of Willie Nelson.

Well, we're havin' a happy birthday.
Happy birthday to me and you.
I believe it's our seventeenth birthday.
You know it's come at last, you do.
And when you're havin' a happy birthday,
there ain't no time for feelin' blue.

We laughed, we applauded, and Matty popped the cork on a lovely Dom Pérignon. I've never had a birthday half as good. Ever.

It was a beyond-fabulous evening in the Angel household.

I knew I had to cherish it because history had taught me that life could turn completely upside down in the time it took to say "Man, it's really good to be home."

11

Our school bell is a real bell—and it was tolling.

The kids hanging out on the front steps, the knots of girls gathered in the little courtyard between the school and the apartment house next door, and the bunch of boys sitting on the stairs to the rectory, all got to their feet and streamed into All Saints Academy. Thanks to Mrs. Benardete, I joined them.

Footsteps echoed between the stone walls, backpacks thudded to the floor, and chatter bounced around the twelve rows of pews in the nave. I went to the front row, taking my seat on the aisle behind the railing on the right. A second later, I noticed that my dearest enemy, C.P., was sitting across the aisle, with a few kids between us on my left.

Feeling a wave of revulsion at the sight of her, I looked straight ahead and thought about Hugo.

In just a few minutes, my little brother would have to make his public apology to C.P. for punching her. I had told Hugo I would sit directly in his line of vision, and that anytime he looked at me, I would be smiling and giving him a thumbs-up.

He'd said, "If I were you, Tandy, I'd sit in the back so you can make a fast escape."

I couldn't tell if he was joking.

Dr. Oppenheimer came up the right-hand aisle and stood in front of the pulpit, his gaze settling on me for an instant before moving away. He cleared his throat and said, "All right now, everyone. Settle down. This morning, we will hear from Mr. Hugo Angel. He has something he wishes to say."

Heads swiveled to watch Hugo come up the center aisle. He usually wears his hair in a long, rusty mop of curls. But for today, Harry had trimmed Hugo's hair and combed it back.

Hugo had also put aside his daily uniform of jeans and a Giants T-shirt and instead wore a white dress shirt and a pair of blue slacks.

He looked adorably mature.

As he passed my seat on the aisle, I tried to read his

expression, but he was giving nothing away. He climbed the steps and took the pulpit, but given his four-foot-ten-inch height, he didn't exactly tower over it. Still, he had presence.

Oppenheimer said, "Please give Hugo your attention."

Blood rushed to my face. I was anxious for my little brother. Would he embarrass himself? It didn't matter. I would love him no matter what.

Hugo said, "Good morning, God and Dr. Oppenheimer and Claudia and everyone.

"I have something to say. I know it's not right to get physical when all that's happening is name-calling. So, Claudia, I apologize for hitting you yesterday. That was wrong. I lost my temper, and I won't do it again.

"But what *you* did was also wrong. You attacked my sister without provocation. Through no fault of her own, Tandy has been through the seven circles of hell. Our parents recently died, our brother was accused of murder, and it was Tandy who found out the truth and saved us from a lifetime in prison. And, C.P., as her best friend, you know what Tandy has suffered more than anyone. But as a friend who then betrayed my sister in the cruelest way possible, know that one of her circles of hell is entirely inhabited by *you*. Just when you should have been the most supportive, you did everything you could to make Tandy suffer even more. Judging by your behavior yesterday, you're continuing your sick little games even now. For that, you deserve every ounce of her pain, times ten. And I hope you get it.

"So I want to finish by saying please accept my apology for hitting you, C.P. I mean that sincerely. But until you apologize to my sister, I advise you to stay out of the Angels' way. If you see us in the hallway, keep your eyes off us. If you see us in class, don't speak to us. And if we're coming up the stairs, I strongly suggest that you *don't come down.*

"May God bless all the students and faculty of this great school and all the people they love and who love them. Amen."

"Amen" in unison rolled forward from all the rows behind me. And then the most remarkable thing happened. Almost everyone jumped to their feet and applauded, and some even whistled and stamped as Hugo came down from the pulpit.

I grabbed his arm and squeezed it. He grinned and continued up the aisle. I almost expected him to start slapping hands, for people to throw flowers.

It was a true triumph. My little brother, a super kid in every way, had defended my honor and his.

Instinctively, I turned toward C.P. She stood there, glaring, still as a stone, her expression a combination of rage and disbelief. And then I lost sight of her as the boisterous kids spilled out into the aisle.

But I saw enough to know that she was mad, all right. And knowing her as I do, I could tell she wouldn't let this public takedown go unanswered.

Not a chance.

12

After the dismissal bell rang, I took a cab to a gray stone building on William Street in downtown Manhattan where our family friend and lawyer, Philippe Montaigne, has his office.

Phil is one of the good guys, but he is also Uncle Peter's lawyer, and so not above suspicion.

I took the elevator to his suite on the twentieth floor and announced myself to the young woman at the desk. She phoned Phil, and within ninety seconds, he came through the inner door and held out his arms to me.

Phil is a very handsome man. He always looks crisp and smooth in dark suits, his thinning hair shaved short and his skin a warm Caribbean bronze.

Philippe filled a mug for me at the coffee urn and took me into his airy modern office. I sat down in a chair across from his desk, dropped my bag to the floor, and turned my fierce attention on him.

"What's so urgent, Tandy?" he said, getting right to it.

"I have to talk with you about Angel Pharma."

"Okay. I'm listening."

"I saw things when I was in France that prove Angel Pharmaceuticals is a criminal enterprise."

"That's quite an assertion, Tandy. What happened in France?" Phil asked me.

I told our dear family friend the parts of the Paris sojourn that had to do with Angel Pharma. I briefed him about my grandmother's scientific mind, and that she had arrived at formulas to boost intelligence and strength. "But she abandoned these recipes when the animal trials showed her that the effects could be remarkable—but fatal," I explained.

I named names. I cited examples. I told Phil that I had found documents that linked my father and my uncle Peter to the recovery of these formulas for "smart" drugs that had carried lethal side effects. I knew of three boys in France who had died from taking the pills, and I didn't doubt there were countless others.

"You have the documents proving this?"

46

And that was when my agitation overwhelmed my happiness at seeing Phil. He was only asking me a simple question, but it felt like a challenge. I hesitated before speaking again, using a moment to collect my thoughts and calm myself a little.

I took a breath before saying, "The documents were destroyed when Gram Hilda's house was set on fire. But I have anecdotal evidence. *Good* evidence.

"Phil, my brothers and I took these drugs our whole lives. You might say we benefited from them; it's true that we test very high in intelligence and physical skills. But based on what happened to other test subjects, we could be *dying*.

"Meanwhile, Peter Angel is still exporting pretty pills with poetic names as candied vitamins. It's immoral, unethical, and has got to be illegal. Phil, you believe me, don't you?"

My anger had been surging as I spoke. I hadn't quite managed to keep it out of my voice.

"Tandy, Tandy, please calm down," said Phil. I saw concern in his face, and I trusted his sincerity. But I couldn't calm down. I felt frantic and frustrated and afraid that he wouldn't take me seriously.

"Your doctors have given you full batteries of tests, and you're in the top one percent of perfect health," he said.

My God, I wanted to scream bloody hell. I clenched my fists and bit my lip, and I felt sweat dripping into my eyes.

Phil said reasonably, "And to your main point, Tandy, you understand, you can't close down a corporation with undocumented anecdotes that are legally ancient and took place in another country."

Lights flashed in front of my eyes, and I found it hard to breathe. I grabbed the edge of the desk and tried to plant my suddenly weightless feet on the floor.

What was wrong with me?

Was it my newfound righteous anger blazing along my neural pathways that was making me feel this light-headed? Was my anger actually running the rest of me?

Or was I having symptoms of an early, pill-induced fatal illness? I tried to swallow. I licked my dry lips, and I stood up straight.

"I don't care about what we can't do, dammit!" I shouted, leaning over the desk to get right in his face. "Do not try to pacify me. No one is tracking these drugs. No one knows what is becoming of the people taking them. I can't sit by and let this happen.

"And neither should you."

I smiled into his shocked face and sat down. "Now, where do we begin?"

CONFESSION

At night, when I'm alone in bed and I finally allow the cold loneliness to steal over me, my thoughts always, *always* turn to James.

Our feelings had been so strong, they had broken through my pill-induced emotional coma and had overcome the unbelievable obstacles our parents had piled between us.

It was just a few months ago that I had reunited with James in, appropriately, the most romantic city in the world. We'd spent a magical evening exploring Paris together, giddily drunk on wine and love. Later, in a tiny and shabby Parisian hotel, James and I had finally, fully, become one. It was the most incredible night of my life.

The next day would be the most devastating.

By the time I woke up, James was gone. His cowardly good-bye note made me question everything and answered nothing. And the next time I saw James, he had just slept with my best friend.

Less than an hour after I had bitch-slapped C.P. and slammed the door in James's face, his horrible and extremely powerful father was dead, just after he had shot my driver in the head. His car had crashed into a tree while trying to run mine off the road.

Soon after Royal Rampling's death, my uncle Peter bought back the controlling shares of Angel Pharmaceuticals from Rampling's estate. I knew it had to have been done with James's blessing. He had hated his father but had already admitted that he had no intention of giving up his father's money, even for me.

When I think about that, my brain seizes up in a blind, wordless *fury*.

But despite all the ways that James had used and betrayed me, I confess that a loathsome little part of my heart wouldn't stop longing for him.

I daydreamed about his smile. The way he loved to stroke my hair. His casual references to our future together. Every single time he told me he loved me.

And in the safety of darkness, like now, I can't stop myself from recalling—in excruciating detail—everything we had done that night in Paris.

And despising myself for every aching thrill I felt.

13

I coped with my first chaotic week at school, avoiding C.P. by keeping to the outer passageways of the school between classes and studying in the isolated choir loft. I even got praise from Dr. Oppenheimer for a succinct description of chaos theory.

But underneath the appearance of normality, I hadn't forgotten my new mission in life.

I *burned* with it.

On Friday, the school day ended at last, and Leo was waiting for me at the curb. I got into the car and turned my thoughts to the meeting ahead, and after fifteen minutes of stop-and-go traffic on Forty-Second Street, Leo dropped me off in front of the iconic Chrysler Building.

By then, my mind was totally focused. I went through a revolving door that released me into the building's marbled lobby and found Philippe Montaigne staring up at the gorgeous Art Deco murals on the thirty-foot ceilings.

I tapped my lawyer on the shoulder. We hugged, then grabbed an open elevator. As the car rose toward the nineteenth floor, Phil said, "Let me do the talking."

"I'll do my best, but I'm under a lot of pressure, Phil," I said. "You could say that my purpose in life is about to culminate here and now."

"Please, for your own sake, keep your expectations in check, Tandy."

Before I could say, "Me? Never," the elevator doors slid open into a spacious reception area and we were shown to a glassed-in conference room, where six gray-haired, gray-suited lawyers and my paunchy, ginger-haired uncle Peter sat around a marble conference table.

I could see Peter's pink little eyes behind his glasses. Because of his porky looks, we kids had called him Uncle Pig most of our lives.

Maybe that was one of the reasons he hated us. But it wasn't the only one. Once, when I was younger, I had even asked him.

"Because the whole snotty pack of you are revolting. Especially you."

Now he smiled broadly upon seeing me. He was putting on a show. "How are we feeling, Tandoori? All better now? All your marbles accounted for? Got new bulbs in your chandelier?"

"I'm fine, Uncle Peter. And how is your worldwide reputation for limitless corruption and deplorable greed faring?" I smiled venomously as I took the seat opposite my uncle, with Phil to my right.

Peter sarcastically introduced me around as his brother Malcolm's daughter. "Tandoori is named for an Indian cooking oven."

When the snickers and introductions had ceased, Phil said, "My client is the victim of Angel Pharmaceuticals products. We're here to serve notice that if your vitamin division is not voluntarily closed down until independent scientists can study your product line, we will notify the FDA, the FBI, the IRS, and Interpol regarding the questionable ingredients in those so-called vitamins."

There was a moment of stunned silence, which I enjoyed. We'd caught Angel Pharma napping. I was prepared for anything, or so I thought, until all the lawyers started barking like hyenas.

"If I may address my niece," said Uncle Pig.

Phil said, "Address *me*, Peter."

Ignoring him, Peter stood up, walked around to my side

of the table, and stabbed the air with his forefinger, *this close* to my nose.

Reflexively, I rolled my chair back.

Peter's spittle sprayed my face as he hissed. "Because of those pills, you're as healthy as a cow and more intelligent than you were ever meant to be. And in all these years, you've never shown a smidgen of gratitude for your extraordinary life, you little *shit*."

From the murderous look in his eyes, it was clear he was more than willing to end my extraordinary life right then and there.

14

I was stunned by Peter's vehemence and audacity. It was as if he had actually taken a sledgehammer to my heart.

I fumbled for a comeback and was coming up with nothing when luckily Phil picked up where Peter had left me for dead.

Phil said, "We can prove that children who were given those so-called vitamins aged rapidly and died before their twentieth birthdays. My client is seventeen."

"Please provide evidence of this fairy tale," Peter said. "I wager that you cannot, because it is one hundred percent pure bull crap, not to mention outrageously libelous. Allow me to confer with my lawyers."

The hyenas barked some more, saying sarcastically how

scared they were of what I could do to the company. They thought they were hilarious but obviously were not funny at all.

Phil went on, "As I was saying, Peter, we can do this the easy way. You agree to discontinue all shipments of your products until independent scientists we approve have analyzed the ingredients. Or we will notify the agencies I mentioned, and my client and her brothers will sue for damages. They will sue *you*, Peter, personally."

"We're not discontinuing a damned thing, so do your worst," Peter spat. "In fact, we have a boatload heading for Shanghai tomorrow morning. As for you, you little snot," he said, turning to me, "you've got nothing on me. I can't wait to wipe the courtroom floor with your nasty little face."

I'd been seething since Uncle Pig became my guardian. I'd kept myself under control for most of the last year, but now the dam that had been holding back my fury burst wide open.

I stood up with my backpack and unzipped it. A flood of candy-colored pills poured out across the conference table, causing the lawyers to recoil in surprise.

The pills were beautiful, not just because they were of every shape and color. They were beautiful because they were evidence, and because every single one of them was stamped with the name and logo of Angel Pharmaceuticals.

"I've got nothing on you?" I said into Peter's startled face. "I've got *everything*, Uncle. I can't wait to bring this evidence to court so the whole world will know that you're a soulless maniac who has caused irreparable damage to your own flesh and blood.

"You had full knowledge that these pills are dangerous and even lethal but freely gave them to us anyway. For all I know, you may have already killed us."

15

Pills continued to cascade off the long marble table and onto the floor as I walked briskly out of the conference room with Philippe right behind me. I fixed my expression into a mask of supreme indifference. But in truth, I was scared and furious. My heart was like a fire hose pumping hot, adrenalized blood through my veins.

Phil pushed the button for the elevator and said, "Think about this carefully, Tandy. Going head-to-head with Peter when he is fighting for his life is going to be a nuclear war. *Everyone* is going to get dragged through the mud. Are you sure you want me to proceed with this action?"

Phil looked very concerned. And I understood what he was telling me. Before the case was over, injuries would be inflicted on both sides, and not just to me. My brothers would go through the grinder as well.

But I had a firm belief that right was might and that we would beat Peter and shut down his corrupt, child-killing drug factory. It was a fight worth fighting.

"The company may try to negotiate," Phil told me as Leo opened the car door for me. "He doesn't want the FDA poking into his laboratory, that's for sure."

"You know Peter. You think he'll negotiate?"

"Not a chance," he admitted.

"He may try to shut me up permanently," I said. "There have been several attempts on my life in the last year, like the fire that torched Gram Hilda's house in Paris. But I'm willing to risk everything to have Angel Pharma shut down, so help me God."

"A good reason to keep your head down. On the other hand, you could win tens of millions in damages."

I barely heard what he was telling me. I said, "Phil, I'm officially authorizing you to file a complaint against Angel Pharmaceuticals. As soon as possible."

As we left the building, I said good-bye to my lawyer and put on my shades. After Leo locked me inside our bulletproof car, we headed uptown, and I thought about the elements of our case.

Charts had once existed of the Angel kids' drug protocols.

There were memos and documents and reports, cartons of them. And there were inquiries from other governments that saw the military potential of Angel Pharma's products, thanks to the mind-boggling results from physical examinations done on Matty and Hugo.

Unfortunately, this rich stash of incriminating evidence had burned up in the fire in Paris, but Hugo, Harry, Matty, and I were alive. And we could testify to the effects of Angel Pharma's so-called vitamins on us—if we lived that long.

I was abruptly brought back into the moment when the car stopped in the familiar semicircular driveway.

I asked, "Leo, do you have a license to carry?"

"Yes. I'm armed at all times: gun, knife, and hands. I'm a master of MMA."

"Good."

"I also have eyes in the back of my head."

He took off his cap, and two piercing blue eyes that were tattooed on the back of his shaved scalp stared me down.

Leo's reflection winked at me in the rearview mirror. I laughed and said, "I'll be down in forty-five minutes."

Leo opened the car door for me, and I marched up the steps and through the front doors of Waterside.

16

I took a chair in the anteroom of Dr. Robosson's office. I crossed my legs and pulled on my hair as the standard "Be Happy" music played through the speakers and the familiar fragrances of lilac and lemon balm came through the ventilators. Nothing had changed a bit in the week since I'd left Waterside.

But *I* felt different.

I no longer resided here and was neither confined nor protected by the high granite walls and the hundreds of caregivers at this place.

I was thinking of my lounge chair in the solarium overlooking the river when voices came through the door:

Dr. Robosson's warm tones, interspersed with a man's gravelly "Good-bye. See you tomorrow, Doctor R."

The door swung open. A hunched, barefoot man in a terry-cloth robe shuffled out, and Dr. Robosson invited me in.

She was wearing a rosy pink suit and smiled broadly as I went to the chair across from her larger one. She closed the door, and when she was seated, she gave me a long look—what I call an eyeball diagnosis. Then she said, "How have you been, Tandy?"

I burst into tears.

Oh, man, I was not ready for that.

Dr. Robosson looked terribly worried as she passed me the tissue box. I pulled out a wad and sobbed into them. When I'd pretty much cried myself out, Dr. Robosson said, "Tandy? What's happened? What's hurting you?"

For some reason, I found this hilarious, and so a couple more of my precious forty-five minutes were spent dissolved in hysterical laughter. Oh my God. It felt so good to laugh.

Dr. Robosson waited me out, and when I was truly ready to begin my session, I said, "Nothing is hurting me, Dr. Robosson. It's just that I'm so relieved to see you."

Her face relaxed. She smiled and leaned back in her chair. "I missed you, too."

I laughed again. Look, I know I was somewhat hysterical. And then I blurted, "Dr. Robosson, the new apartment is wonderful. I have a beautiful room, and our lawyer tracked down a lot of our old furniture and bought it back for us."

"That must feel pretty good," said my doctor.

I nodded, and she asked me what else was on my mind. It felt great just sitting across from her familiar face and nurturing presence.

I said, "That first morning, when I went back to school, C.P. was on the front steps, almost like she was waiting for me to show up."

"I see. Tell me more about that."

"It was horrible. She attacked me from the first word, as if *she* was the one who was betrayed. I stood up for myself, believe me, but it was a ridiculous fight. And then Hugo punched C.P. in the stomach."

"*Oh.* What happened then?"

"The headmaster stepped in and told Hugo he had to apologize to C.P. in front of the whole student body."

"Oh, wow. How did that go?"

"Amazing. He made his apology and then absolutely tore her down, and got everyone in the school on his side in the process. He finished to standing applause. For an apology!"

Dr. Robosson laughed appreciatively and said, "You seem very proud of him."

"I am. I love my little brother so much, and I'm even a little jealous of how he takes on a world in which he can hardly control a thing. And he just kills it."

Dr. Robosson smiled. "It's safe to say your days of having the emotional range of a robot are over."

I grinned.

Dr. Robosson shot a glance at the little red clock on her side table and said, "Our session is almost up. Shall we meet again, same time next week?"

"Oh, Dr. Robosson, I have to tell you this one more thing. I went to Angel Pharmaceuticals with my lawyer today. And we stood up to my uncle Peter and his gang of legal thugs. We said either he had to stop shipping the pills or I'd sue him for the damages. Big-time."

"Tandy. You waited until this minute to tell me that?"

"I'm wondering if my parents would be furious with me. Or if they'd be proud," I said.

She said, "They'd be proud. But those are both big subjects. Let's spend some time on this next week, okay? And try to remember your dreams."

I found Leo watching birds with a pair of binoculars. He opened the car door, and I got into the backseat knowing that my frontal attack on Angel Pharma was all I'd be thinking about until I saw Dr. Robosson again.

17

When I *walked into the apartment* that late afternoon, it was as though I had stepped into the path of a cyclone, one of those twisters that sound like a runaway freight train headed right at you.

It was *insane*.

Everyone was in the living room. Even my mother's prized sculpture, Robert, had been pulled with his recliner up to the television.

Matthew was lying on the sofa, feet pointed at the football game. He had jacked up the sound to headache-loud. Judging by the number of bottle caps on the coffee table and beer bottles on the floor, Matty and Robert had been partying for a long while.

Jacob was yelling something to Matthew that I couldn't make out.

Hugo was curled up in the Pork Chair, hugging his knees, and from the way his chest was heaving, I knew he was crying his heart out.

Harry was twenty feet away, playing his piano as if he was the only one in the room. I didn't recognize the tune, but it was something military, with menacing thrumming and sharp notes cutting through the sound of cheering fans from the TV.

I yelled, "What's going on?"

Uncle Jacob held up a newspaper, one of the New York City daily tabloids. The headline took up half the page.

ANGEL IS DEVIL IN DISGUISE

"Have you seen this?" Jacob shouted. He shook the paper, and the inside pages broke loose and fluttered onto the floor—all but the front page, which Jacob gripped tightly in both hands.

I said, "No, what is it?"

I eased the front page out of Jacob's grasp and scrutinized the photo. It was Matty's Tesla, and it looked like it had rear-ended a van. Matty was being helped out of his car by two uniformed cops. Blood was running down his face.

Now I looked at Matty in the flesh. Both of his eyes were black and blue, and some of his hair had been shaved, with stitches visible in his scalp.

There was pounding on the ceiling: our upstairs neighbor registering a complaint. By then, Jacob had clearly overshot his limit. He bellowed at my twin, "*Stop!*"

The piano cut out instantly.

Jacob found the remote under the pile of Cheetos bags and switched off the TV.

"Sit up," he said to Matthew. "Right now."

"Christ," said Matty. "I'm watching the game."

And now we were all watching *him*. He had a ferocious "don't even *think* of messing with me" look on his face that I'd seen many times before—usually when he was running with a ball under his arm and was returning a kickoff through enemy lines.

But that expression crumpled as Matty sat up abruptly and put his feet on the floor.

"I got cut from the team, all right? I'm out of a job. I didn't want to tell anyone until I got a new deal."

Hugo got out of the chair, climbed onto the couch, and threw his arms around Matty's neck.

"They're crazy!" Hugo cried. "They can't fire you, Matty. They need you."

Matthew said, "Sorry, buddy. I violated my contract. People get cut from ball clubs all the time. It's just the first time for me." He lowered his eyes to the floor. His wretched form radiated shame and misery.

Would our family's pain ever stop?

18

The sudden silence seemed to have a vibration of its own. Since I'd walked into the apartment, the sun had dropped below the horizon. Without the TV on, the apartment was nearly dark. And now the vignette on the red sofa had the look of a surrealist painting.

The three of them were a study in pain.

Hugo stood on the sofa, bouncing with a nervous energy and listening intently. Jacob sat in the chair, leaning toward Matty. He still held the paper in his hand.

Jake said, "Matthew, don't you think you owe us an explanation?"

Matty's voice cracked when he said, "There's no one to blame but me."

He dropped his head into his hands and began to cry. This was freaking heartrending. Matty hadn't cried when our parents died. He hadn't cried when his girlfriend was horribly killed or when he was charged with her murder.

I don't remember *ever* seeing Matthew cry.

Jacob went over to the sofa and put his arm around Matty's shoulder. He said, "Take it easy. Just talk to us."

"Don't be nice to me, okay?" Matty said.

He broke into a new round of sobbing, and then, when he'd caught his breath, he said, "What happened was—I got loaded. I was leaving a club in Brooklyn. There were girls. They're always around me, you know, Jake? They climbed into the car without asking, and sure, I thought, why the hell not?

"And then one of them was kissing my ear, and the music was blasting and I was drinking Stoli out of the bottle and I lost control of the car and I ran into a parked van.

"It added up to nothing. *Nothing.* No one was hurt. Not badly. One of the girls has a broken arm. She's seventeen. I didn't check her ID when she got into my car, you know?

"I bailed myself out this morning and then...and then I got cut from the team, and because of that, my reality show was canceled. And so that you know *everything*, I also lost my savings," he said. "All of it. I made a risky investment. That's why I got loaded in the first place."

I expected Jacob to ask about the injured girl, to say something about the DWI or the legal implications of the accident, but he said, "You mean you're broke?"

"Yeah. Except for the pittance from Gram Hilda's estate. I can't live on that—I'm officially busted."

"You can forget that 'pittance,' too, now," Jacob said in disgust. "There was *one* condition on your inheritance. One. 'Don't disgrace the family name.' And here it all is. Drunk driving, teenage girl injured, fired from the team, and who knows what kind of lawsuits are coming.

"This whole mess is now global entertainment news. TMZ to the moon. You'll be getting a notice from the trustee, if you haven't already. Check your e-mail."

"I lost my phone."

Harry laughed at that one. He'd lost a lot of phones himself. But Hugo, Jacob, and I stared at Matthew in disbelief. I was shocked that his fantastic, enviable life had fallen apart in just one day. What had made him so reckless? I'd already surmised that his anger problem was caused by the drugs, but maybe they'd affected his judgment in the long term, too. How would we ever know?

Jacob had worked himself into a fury all over again.

Standing over my oldest brother, he said, "Okay, Matthew. I want you to listen carefully. Unlike your siblings, you're an adult. You're going to have to pull yourself out of this mess. It's the only way you'll recover your reputation and self-esteem. There will be no freeloading; you'll find no safety net here."

Hugo got between Matthew and Jacob and shouted at Jacob. "He's our brother first, last, and always, Jake! Don't you dare talk to him that way or I'll punch you in the nose."

Matthew stood up and, looking more like a homeless man than a celebrated all-star athlete, headed to the doorway.

"There won't be any more trouble, Jake," he said. "Bye, kids."

Hugo cried out, "Matty, don't go!"

But the door closed, leaving only the memories of the terrible scene still hanging in the air around us.

"He's family," Harry said to Jacob. "We take care of our own." I agreed with Harry and Hugo.

Jacob said, "He's been looking for a way to crash, and now he's done it in every sense of the word. I won't have him bringing down the three of you."

"We can take care of ourselves," I spat.

"When you're twenty-one, you can take care of yourself. For now, you have me," Jacob returned.

I tossed my head as if I still had long hair, then spun around and headed up the stairs to my room with Hugo on my heels. Harry went back to the piano and ran the scales listlessly in the dark.

So much for a pleasant family evening.

I wondered if there would ever be peace and harmony in the house of Angels again.

19

About an hour after Matthew left our apartment, Jacob knocked on our bedroom doors and summoned us to dinner.

It was a tense, overcooked meal of chicken, string beans, and potatoes that was interrupted several times by texts and phone calls to Jacob, which he took out of earshot.

"Hey," said Hugo as Jacob began clearing the table. "I'm not done with my pudding."

"Sorry," said Jacob. "And I'm sorry I yelled, but Matthew is almost twenty-five. He must account for his actions. And he will. The girl in the car with him, Sandra Rendell, is filing a lawsuit. He has a DWI, and it's not his first. Matthew's insurance will pay for the cars, but not for the fear and emotional trauma he caused a number of people, some of whom are opportunists. And since Matthew is broke, I honestly don't know what he's going to do."

My heart was banging almost louder than the dishes and cutlery Jacob was taking to the kitchen. I wished I could close my eyes, click my heels, and go back to our wonderful homecoming birthday party with cake and gag gifts and singing.

Nice thought, but no. I was still at the horrid dinner table. Sometimes there's nothing you can do about timing.

"Jacob, I need to have a family discussion on a different subject entirely."

Jacob sat back down at the dining table, which had been bought new and had no memories attached. But I would say there were enough memories among those of us at the table to populate a war museum.

My brothers and Jacob turned to me, and out came my opening line.

"I hired Philippe to represent me against Angel Pharmaceuticals and Uncle Peter, personally, for damages because of the pills. Me and anyone else in this family who wants to join me."

"I'll back you up," said Harry. "I don't know if I'm damaged, but I'm not what anyone calls normal."

"Sign me up, too," said Hugo uneasily. "I know I'm a little messed up in my head."

That broke my heart.

"Phil says you have a case?" Jacob asked me.

"He does."

I sounded completely sane to my own ears when I said, "I've always known I was meant to do something important with my life, and now I know what it is. I have to put Angel Pharmaceuticals out of business.

"And you, Uncle Jake, more than anyone else, know why."

20

I was in my new room, which reminded me so much of the old one. Same blue walls, my desk under the window, and lights from the city and the traffic below casting rays and moving shadows on the ceiling.

I should have felt comforted by the familiarity and safety of home, but I couldn't sleep.

I thought of the elderly couple Jacob had taken me to meet in France, sweet people whose children had taken Angel Pharma pills at the behest of my uncle Peter.

I remembered the photo of the three boys, who had been cheerful and ordinary in the best possible way, until their parents had been seduced by promises that their children could be extraordinary—talented, brilliant, athletic geniuses. All they had to do was take the pills, keep records, and send the reports to Peter Angel.

That was ten years ago. Those boys were long dead.

But I knew their names.

I knew how to find their parents again.

I thought about the time my brothers and I had gone to see Peter at the factory in Hell's Kitchen. We had seen forklifts moving wooden crates into position for shipping. We had read the names stenciled on the crates: STRONG AS OX. MORE BEAUTIFUL THAN PEONY. VERY SMART CHILDREN. NO WORRIES.

These were the same pills we had taken, but they had been renamed for the Chinese markets.

The memory of that enormous warehouse filled with millions of pills sent rage ripping through me again. If I didn't stop Peter, I was as complicit and as responsible as he was.

I was so fiercely engaged in my own thoughts that my phone buzzed several times before I realized it.

I grabbed my phone and said hello.

"Tandy. It's Katherine."

My God. My God.

Hearing her voice was so shocking, but also delicious and amazing. It was as if I had stepped out of my body into lightness and something like hope. For so long, I'd thought Katherine was dead. Then, only three months ago, she had astonishingly found me in Paris.

How had she come back to life? It was impossible—and yet it was true. It was her voice, her face, and she was completely material. My sister, Katherine, who had been dead for six years, was *alive*.

The experience of walking with her for an unforgettable hour had been surreal. I couldn't stop staring at her. I had known all the details of her death, and I had mourned her for so long that of course I doubted my sanity.

But I wasn't crazy. Katherine, my wonderful big sister, hadn't come out of the shadows just to say hello. She had come to warn me that my life and the lives of our brothers were in danger. And she had made me promise to forget about her, saying, "Your safety and mine depend on keeping our meeting a secret."

Still, I'd told Harry. I'd told Jacob.

And then I'd tried to forget my only sister.

That had been excruciating, but never mind. She was calling me. I screamed her name, then belatedly covered my mouth. It was a big apartment, but it wasn't soundproof.

"Tandy, Tandy, how are you?"

"No, you first," I said. "Tell me about you!"

"I suppose that's fair, Tandoo. After all, I'm calling you. But I can only say that I am happy. So please tell me about you. I'm dying to hear some news."

I told Katherine I had checked out of Waterside, and, ignoring the C.P. drama, I gave her some of the brighter notes of my return to big-city life. But in the end, my new lifetime occupation jumped out of my mouth.

"I'm taking Peter to court. I'm going to stop him from pushing the damned pills, Katherine. I'm going to shut him down. And I'm going to make him pay."

There was a long silence. I could almost hear her thoughts wafting toward me over thousands of miles of ocean, though I had no idea where she really lived.

"Katherine?"

"Tandy. I'm here."

Her voice had lost its shimmer. I held the phone with both hands.

"What's wrong, Kath? You agree, don't you? In fact, I was thinking maybe you could give a deposition."

"Tandy, no. You have to stop. Did you forget everything I told you? You don't want to go against Peter. It's danger-ous for every single one of us."

There was a crackle on the line, and then a beep that told me we had been disconnected. Fear for her safety swamped me. I did every kind of search and operator-assisted redial, and when I couldn't reach Katherine, I put my phone on my chest and turned off the lights.

When I woke up in the morning, I hadn't moved at all. The phone was exactly where I had placed it.

Katherine hadn't called me back.

CONFESSION

When I was little, I adored my sister, Katherine, more than anyone else in the world. She was gentle and kind—two qualities sorely lacking in my parents—and she was the one I ran to when I needed comforting. I wanted to be just like her, in every way.

Then we found out she'd been killed in an accident abroad.

And it was all because of Peter.

He was our uncle, older than our father. But somehow, he had developed a sick obsession with my sister—his *niece*—when she was just a child. He had openly hated the rest of us but indulged Katherine by buying her gifts, taking her out for treats, making her sit on his lap. God knows what else.

In the basement of Gram Hilda's house, I discovered repulsive love letters my uncle had written to my sister when she was still a teenager. I imagine she felt helpless to stop him, with our parents not exactly being the supportive type.

So when the opportunity presented itself, she took the only way out.

When Katherine was sixteen, my parents gave her a trip to South Africa as a special reward for being accepted at MIT. Ever the genius, she successfully faked her own death and went into hiding, never making it known to us that she was still alive for fear that Peter would find her. Even now, years later, she couldn't reveal herself because she was terrified of what he would do to her.

My beautiful, smart, promising sister—now a refugee from her own family.

So if you want to know the real reason for my crusade to burn Angel Pharma to the ground, it's simple.

Peter Angel.

I want to destroy him for what he did to my sister, my family. Without the money and the prestige that the company affords him, he would be less than nothing. Financially, socially, and professionally, he might as well be dead.

Speaking of dead, you might be wondering why I need to go through the trouble of annihilating Peter through his company, when, for a certain sum of money, I could go the more direct route.

Believe me, friend. It's under careful consideration.

AGAINST
ALL
ODDS

21

The Supreme Court of New York is in a 1920s granite-faced, classical-Roman-style building with a carved pediment and soaring columns standing in the heart of lower Manhattan.

At almost nine o'clock on a Monday morning, as light snow fluttered down on Centre Street, Philippe and his second chair, Drake DiBella, along with my brothers and me, climbed the wide steps to the entrance of the courthouse building.

It was, in the truest sense of the word, *awesome.*

It would be an enormous thing for four kids to take on their parents in a court of law, but this was way more than that. We were taking on our uncle and, by extension, a major corporation. My brothers and I were ready.

I missed Jacob's strong presence, but he was in Paris, fighting to retain Matty's inheritance. Despite our uncle's absence, I felt good. My righteous anger warmed me with steady heat. I was ready for vindication and justice at last.

We climbed an impressive marble staircase to a hallway where uniformed officers opened the doors to courtroom 928. The room where so much would be decided today was imposing and austere. It was paneled in dark wood to shoulder height, with stark, white-painted plaster above the panels, tall windows on one wall, and pendant lights hanging from the ceiling like frozen teardrops.

Only a few dozen people sat in the gallery. The six of us walked up the aisle and through the gate. Chairs scraped as we took our seats at the plaintiff's counsel table.

We had just taken our places when laughter and loud talking rolled up from the back of the room. I recognized Uncle Pig's grunts and the responding barks and yaps of his legal team.

Team Pig went to the counsel table across the aisle from ours. They couldn't have appeared more self-assured. It was as if once this bothersome little proceeding was over they would each get into their private jets and take off to Saint Thomas or Ibiza.

Actually, I might have looked a little smug myself.

We were in the right. We had been criminally used without our knowledge or consent in order to test drugs for commercial purposes. These drugs had altered our brains and actually turned us into freaks.

Since our meeting with Peter's lawyers two weeks ago, Philippe had filed a complaint with the courts and Peter's horrid legal team had moved to dismiss it.

Now the judge would make his decision.

I'd done some research, of course. Judge George Campbell had a reputation for fairness, but that meant he was also known to deep-six frivolous lawsuits. I hoped when he'd listened to both sides, he would do the right thing.

As if the judge had heard my thoughts, he came through a narrow door right behind his bench. He was tall, lanky, and in his midsixties. He had a bit of a smile as he sat down and rolled his chair into position.

The bailiff called the court to order and announced that this was the case of Matthew, Tandoori, Harrison, and Hugo Angel versus Peter Angel and Angel Pharmaceuticals.

Judge Campbell looked down at the papers in front of him, and then he looked up at us. The room seemed to swim as the judge's warm brown eyes connected with mine. I suddenly worried that our claim of abuse might have suffered when translated into legalese.

The judge adjusted his glasses and said, "I've read the complaint filed by the plaintiffs and the motion to dismiss made by the defendants. The court understands that the plaintiffs are aggrieved that their permission wasn't sought before ingesting these performance-enhancing drugs. They were children, and all but one are still children. It would have been prudent and morally correct to wait until they were old enough to agree to take nonessential supplements."

I relaxed my jaw muscles and unclenched my fists. The judge understood how we'd been betrayed and harmed and that Angel Pharmaceuticals had to be stopped.

He turned back to the document in front of him.

"The court finds, however," said the judge, "that even assuming that all the allegations made by the plaintiffs are true, they have not suffered any damages. I'm looking here at four remarkable young people, all of whom are A-plus students, creative in their endeavors and exceedingly capable intellectually. One, in fact, is a celebrated athlete, while another is an acclaimed musical prodigy. I find no scientific evidence to support their claims."

What? What was he saying? It felt as if the floor had tipped sideways, that I was about to pass out.

I grabbed Harry's arm. And although the judge's voice sounded warped and muffled, I forced myself to hear.

Judge Campbell said, "For that reason, the defendant's motion to dismiss is granted—with prejudice."

He removed his glasses and looked straight at me, the warmth gone from his eyes. "That means, children, that you are barred from refiling your claim against the defendants. *Permanently.*"

22

I was in complete shock.

I wasn't even sure I'd really heard what Judge Campbell had said. Did he say we had lost and Peter had won? It was inconceivable.

The judge stood up and headed toward the door behind the bench. He was leaving?

No. This was not happening.

I shot to my feet and called out, "Judge Campbell, please. You're missing the point, Your Honor. Those pills were not approved by the Food and Drug Administration. The pills turned us into *freaks*!"

The judge half turned toward me, and he was scowling.

"You've had your day in court, young lady. I've made a decision. If you don't understand, ask your lawyer to explain. Good-bye. And good luck."

Hugo was trapped between the counsel table and the bar behind him. He picked up his chair and hurled it so that he could get out, screaming, "Judge, listen to her!"

But the judge had slipped through his back door and was gone. I stared for an interminable minute at his empty chair. Then I turned to Phil and shouted at him, "What happened? What the hell just happened?"

Phil put one hand on my shoulder and the other on Hugo's head and said, "It was a summary judgment, Tandoori. It's final. Do you understand the term *with prejudice*? It means we are prohibited from refiling the claim, as he said."

I shouted, "Then you have to file a different complaint! Or come at it from another angle. We can't just let this go."

"We lost, Tandy," Phil said. "This was always going to be down to either a yes or a no. Win or lose. We gave it our best, and the evidence was insufficient. We're done."

I was shaking my head *No, no, no*. I had risked so much by going up against Peter, and I had been so sure that the judge would see how my brothers and I had been used and abused. I just couldn't accept the finality of the judge's decision.

But there was no doubt in Uncle Peter's mind.

He crossed the aisle in two steps and leaned across Philippe to say to me, "Happy now, snot-face? Case closed. You can't win them all, Philippe."

Peter strode up the aisle with his entourage in tow, the sound of his laughter echoing throughout the chamber. I was awash in humiliation.

Why didn't the judge understand what had been done to us?

And then Matty's gigantic face was in front of me.

Matty said, "Sorry, kiddo. We all feel as bad as you do, but it's time to go home."

Harry was urging me to move and Phil was holding out his hand to me, but I snapped again.

I screamed at Phil, "This is *wrong*! The judge made his decision, and he can unmake it."

Police officers were heading toward us. This was more humiliation than even I could stand. I followed Phil up the aisle, through the double courtroom doors, and across the wide mezzanine to the stairs.

Phil's long legs were carrying him quickly down the staircase, and I kept calling him as I trotted to keep up.

He stopped short when we reached the ground level. Now that I was looking directly into his face, I saw how upset he was. It finally hit me that he'd just lost a case, and he cared about that. And he cared about *me*.

Crowds of people streamed around us as we stood on the center medallion in the vast marble floor. Phil said, "There are thousands of lawyers in New York who are looking for work, Tandy, and you can hire any one of them. But I'm telling you that this horse is dead. It doesn't matter how much you beat it, or yell at me.

"If you were my daughter, I would tell you the same thing. It's time to quit. I know it hurts—"

"You think?"

"—but we didn't have a provable case."

He went for the courthouse's main doors with the pack of us following behind him. Outside, snow was falling more thickly than before, and it had a crazy effect on me, like static in my mind.

I watched Phil and his deputy walk swiftly toward a pearl-gray town car. They looked like people in a 1940s black-and-white film. All that was missing were umbrellas turning inside out and hats blowing down the street.

I heard Matty calling me, and I turned to see that my brothers were at the car and Leo was holding open the back door. I must have looked wild.

"You having a heart attack, Ms. Tandy?" Leo asked me.

"No. But thanks for asking."

I flung myself into the car, and my brothers piled in after me. Matty took the jump seat facing us.

I'm sure they all saw the blood in my eyes when I said, "This isn't over. Whatever Phil says, whatever the courts decide, I *will* make Peter pay."

23

I sat between Hugo and Harry in the back of our bullet-proof car. Harry was plugged into his music, Hugo was telling Matty how many pounds he could press, and I was mulling over the bloody beating we'd just taken in court-room 928.

I wasn't raised to lose.

Maud and Malcolm Angel were parental terrorists. They rewarded success with fantastic gifts called Grande Gongos and penalized failure with memorable punishments known as Big Chops.

None of us had been spared, and none of us had been told that we were loved. Ever.

Why were we such remarkably unusual children?

Was it nature, nurture, or pharmaceutical enhancement?

The answer is yes. All three.

What made our parents different from other tiger moms and dads was that they practiced what they preached. Malcolm excelled at one thing—running Angel Pharmaceuticals, which he did all night and all day. Maud walked the razor's edge of high finance, and that stressful work made her largely unforgiving. Her motto was "I'll sleep when I'm dead."

If my parents had still been alive and we'd lost a case of this import, we would all have been Chopped. Big-time.

Trust me, it would have been bad.

I was very quiet as we drove uptown. I was a product of my parents after all. I was coming up with an action plan.

24

Once home, I nuked a burrito and took it upstairs, where I locked myself into the sanctuary of my soft blue bedroom and settled myself down to do research of an urgent kind.

First, I made a list of all the important news outlets and created a spreadsheet with phone numbers and e-mail addresses. I ranked each name on my list according to how willing they might be to run with a juicy scandal.

When my list was solid, I composed a press release that I could personalize to individuals but that was universal enough to go to all the journalists and pundits on my list. It was a script I could read, and I could also send it by e-mail.

This is what I wrote to Dr. Norton Abel, senior science reporter at the *New York Times*.

Dear Dr. Abel:

I have read your articles on psychotropic drugs, and I believe you will be interested in my firsthand account of abuses by a major pharmaceutical company that manufactures powerful drugs disguised as "vitamins."

These drugs were designed to turn ordinary children into geniuses with superior strength and exceptional intellect, but under some circumstances, these pills have caused mental defects and even premature death.

Since this pharmaceutical giant cannot get approval from the FDA, they are marketing these pills overseas, where they are allowed to promote these drugs for use by children without restriction.

Dr. Abel, this is not a joke. I have taken these pills most of my life, and so have my siblings. I've met parents whose children have taken the same pills and have died.

You know of me and my family and our relationship to this corrupt corporation. Please contact me at your earliest convenience so that I may tell you the whole wretched story.

Yours truly,
Tandoori Angel

I called Dr. Abel at the *Times*, and when his assistant said he was out of town, I sent him the e-mail. Then I rewrote the opening and contacted renowned TV doctors Sanjay Gupta, Nancy Snyderman, and Mehmet Oz.

So far, no one had taken my calls, but it was still early in the day. I rewrote the pitch, underscoring the criminal child abuse that my brothers and I had been subjected to, and I called Nancy Grace at HLN.

Child abuse usually made her furious, but again, I was told she wasn't available. I sent her an e-mail, and then I had a brainstorm. I phoned Chloe Rhodes, a reporter at the New York *Daily News*, who had just written that horrible story about Matty's car accident.

Surely she would want an inside scoop on the Angels.

I called. She picked up, and after one full hour on the phone, we were like friends. Rhodes said she'd call me back in an hour—and she did.

"I'm sorry," she said. "I couldn't sell the story to my editor. Without documentation, we could be sued, Tandy."

It was a huge setback, but I didn't have time to whine. I sent a flight of personalized e-mails to West Coast entertainment shows and gossip magazines.

To my profound disbelief, no news service or supermarket tabloid responded. Not one soul in the entire media world even wanted to *interview* me. How could this be true?

Then I finally got it.

Anyone who called Peter Angel to confirm my story and get his side of it was told that I was insane, that I had been institutionalized and defeated in court.

Oh my God. What had I done?

I had been so confident that the truth would win out that I had missed one point entirely. The pundits and reporters I had called had smelled blood, all right. *My blood.*

Why go against the gigantic Angel Pharmaceuticals with only my unsubstantiated word, when they could write about my mental breakdown—which was demonstrably a fact? I'd killed my own credibility. No one would believe anything I said ever again. Anything *any* of us said again.

That hurt too much.

I went down to the kitchen and drank probably too much of a bottle of merlot while standing at the sink. After that, I staggered up the spiral staircase to my room. I wrote DO NOT DISTURB in big black letters on yellow paper and taped it to my door.

Then I fell across my bed and passed out.

25

I was savagely awoken the next morning by Hugo jumping up and down on my bed, announcing, "Tandy, you have to get dressed. Sam's mother died."

"Sam's what?"

It felt like someone was hammering nails into my skull, and Hugo's bouncing was making me sick. It took many splintered sunlit moments to get what he was telling me.

"Stop jumping!"

He threw himself down on top of me.

"We're going to the funeral, Tandy. Matty said so. He chartered a plane."

Samantha Peck had been my mom's personal assistant. She lived with us for several years and had been a great friend to us all. We didn't know until after Maud died that Sam was my mother's lover. After my parents' funeral, Sam moved out and Uncle Pig moved in, just when we needed her the most and needed him the *least*.

"What happened to Sam's mom?" I asked.

Hugo shrugged. "I think it was old age. Listen, get dressed. We have to leave."

Ninety minutes later, my three brothers and I were locked and loaded into a small single-engine Pilatus aircraft taking off from New Jersey's Teterboro Airport, heading north to Lake Placid, New York.

The plane was sturdy and elegant, and the pilot introduced himself as "Thomas Trotti. Call me Tom."

Tom was in uniform; he had longish blond hair under his hat, a dimple in each cheek, and a spray of lines at the outer corners of his eyes.

The takeoff got my blood motoring and actually lifted my crappy mood. Once we were airborne, Tom said through the mic, "Folks, it'll be an easy-breezy fifty-five-minute flight, which includes a breathtaking view over the Adirondacks. Because it's such a short hop, we'll only be flying at ten thousand feet, cruising at two hundred seventy knots. What a beautiful day to fly."

It *was* a beautiful day: crisp and clear with a lavender-blue-and-white sky. Matty sat at the window to my left, and Hugo and Harry took the two-seater on the other side of the narrow aisle.

We'd unboxed our snacks and beverages and had been in flight for about forty minutes when something changed—and it felt terribly wrong.

I grabbed Matty's arm and said, "Did you feel that?"

"Yes. The engine cut out," he said. "Don't worry. The pilot can bring it back to life."

I didn't believe Matty. I *knew* he was wrong.

Up ahead, there was frantic action in the cockpit. Red lights flashed on the control panel, accompanied by a rhythmic beeping alarm. Tom was throwing levers and speaking into his headset.

I shouted, "*Tom*, what's happening?"

Our pilot said tersely, "Excuse me, but no talking, please."

Harry and Hugo were awake and looking petrified as the plane not only decelerated but was now sailing downward at a ten-degree angle. Without an engine, we were a giant glider—without power, and maybe without a prayer.

I broke out in a sweat over my entire body.

I thought, *Okay, okay, okay, the engine will catch in a moment*—but it did *not*.

Matty groaned. "This is my fault. Why did I have to book this plane? Oh, God, oh, God. Tandy. Forgive me."

"This is not the end," I told my brothers as we went into an even steeper descent. "We're going to make it."

That was when Hugo screamed.

26

"Mommmmmyyyy!" *Hugo screamed shrilly. It shattered* my heart to hear his fear.

I turned to see him and Harry, but I couldn't reach them, touch them, kiss them, do anything to make them less afraid.

Matty bellowed at the pilot, "Do something, dammit!"

Captain Tom shouted back, "Assume brace position, sir! And shut the hell up."

Matty gripped my hand too hard. It didn't matter. I was sure that in seconds we were going to crash and burn to death, which was the worst possible way to die.

The visceral memories of a different fire swamped me now: the darkness, the fight for air, the choking, the burning in my lungs, and the fierce scalding heat on my face as my nerves shrank back from the flames eating through my grandmother's house in Paris.

I thought, *God, I don't want to die.*

Please. Not us. Not Hugo.

While we were still in the grip of the sickening downward pressure, time stretched out to the horizon. I waited for the shattering moment of impact. How long does it take to fall ten thousand feet? Somewhere, in that time between a split second and an eternity, I lost hope.

There was no way out. No parachute or ejection seat or hand of God to pluck up the plane before it was dashed to the ground.

Shadows flashed across the windows: white, black, white, black again; a stroboscopic light show of trees and sky and snow. Tom was talking gibberish into his headset, probably Maydays and our coordinates to alert rescuers to the fireball we were about to become.

I locked eyes for a moment with Harry, my twin. He reached out his hand, and with tremendous effort against physical forces, we touched fingers. And then he bent over his knees and interlaced his hands behind his neck.

As if that would do any good against what was coming.

I pulled my hand from Matty's and braced, too.

Even though it was hopeless, I prayed. *Please, God, forgive me for whatever I've done and please don't let it hurt.*

And then I felt a noticeable change in our angle of descent. I looked up to see Tom hauling back on the yoke. As the plane leveled out a bit, I saw our crash path through the forest in the narrow slice of windscreen. The thick woods were wall-to-wall evergreens coated with yesterday's snow. But there, between the trees, was a straight patch of snow, like a ski trail.

The pilot yelled, "*BRAAAAAACCCCE!*"

I hugged my knees and closed my eyes and felt the plane smash into the evergreens. Trunks whumped the belly of the plane; then there were more violent bumps and crunches, accompanied by a horrid scraping and ripping sound from my side of the aircraft.

We rolled violently to the left, and I was slammed against Matty and the armrest. I heard my own scream, as if it was coming out of the top of my head.

We hit something unyielding. Like stone.

Matty cried out in agony. How badly was he hurt? I opened my eyes, but then the plane twisted violently around and we were skidding, sliding to the loud, high-pitched screeching of shearing metal.

I screamed, "*Mattyyy!*" but all I heard was another

ripping noise that lasted longer than the first. Out the window I could see the wing being torn from the right side of the plane.

The smell of jet fuel permeated the cabin.

Gasoline.

It was going to happen now. We were all going to burn.

This was my last living moment.

27

Jacob was sitting in a chair beside the bed when I came out of the dark.

Was this real? Or had I passed into death, with Jacob the image left in my mind?

"Uncle Jake?"

He reached for me, hugging me so gently I wasn't sure he'd actually touched me, but I was in his arms anyway.

"Tandy, Tandy, my dear heart. I want to hold you, but I don't want to hurt you."

"I'm alive?"

Our voices sounded very soft and far away.

Jacob sat back in his chair. He put his hands over his

eyes and sobbed. I'd never heard Jacob cry. I wasn't sure I was hearing it now.

I made a few false starts before I was able to ask, "How is...everyone? Are they...alive?"

"Everyone survived. You were lucky, Tandy. All of you."

The hospital room was faintly lit by a crack of light under the door and the glow of the vital signs monitor just to my right.

I smelled antiseptic and had to double-check with my brain that it was not gasoline. And at the same time, I realized that I hurt *everywhere*. I was a great throbbing mass of pain, but as constant and pervasive as the pain was, it was muted.

Whatever drugs were coming through my IV, they were definitely working. I had enough doped-up presence of mind to ask Jacob, "How lucky were my brothers?"

"Matthew's left femur is broken."

I couldn't hear for a moment, and then I asked, "Will he be able to play ball?"

"It's too soon to know."

Jacob's voice was cutting in and going out. I heard, "Hugo and Harry...soft tissue bruising...no head or internal injuries...Thank God."

My monitor beeped as my heart rate picked up. Joy that my brothers were alive. Sadness for Matty, who'd already had enough sadness. And something like hope for myself.

I wiggled my toes. I wasn't paralyzed. I wasn't in bandages. I wasn't burned. *I wasn't burned.* But the plane was still tumbling. I could feel it, skidding, slamming into trees, rolling over and over.

"And Tom?"

"He's going to make it. His family is with him now."

I lost track of time.

When I came back to myself, Jake was talking about the crash, saying Tom had found a short, narrow ridge where he took a chance on a belly landing. We were low enough, going slow enough, and he was pilot enough.

"What guts. What skill," Jacob said.

I heard him say that medevac had arrived within minutes, assessed us, and brought us directly to New York Hospital.

Jacob said, "I wanted you here."

With the pain pulsing softly in the background, my mind set out on several different tracks. I remembered black cars on a beach six months ago. I remembered being kidnapped and locked up and electroshocked until my brain was wiped clean.

I remembered the scorching house fire and the armed cars that had followed me and the gunfire from men who wanted to kill me. I had gotten warnings and threats from friends and enemies. And I could still hear Katherine pleading with me to lie low because we were all in danger.

Nausea surged, violently. I leaned over the bed rail, and Jacob had a pail ready. He held my hot forehead with his cool hand and said, "I've got you, Tandy."

I heaved up nothing and then, panting, I collapsed back into the bed just as nauseated as before.

A nurse appeared. I'd never seen him before. Who was he?

"Time to go to sleep, Ms. Angel."

"Jacob?"

"I hear you, Tandy. I'll be here when you wake up."

A needle went into the tube in my arm.

I said to my commando uncle, "That plane...shouldn't have gone down. Right, Jacob...?"

If he answered, I didn't hear him. I was asleep.

28

I woke up to snow sheeting sideways outside my hospital window. It was good to see all that white, my friend. It was like fresh paint covering up the remains of the terror.

Where was Uncle Jacob?

I turned from the hypnotic snowfall and punched on the TV. I clicked on six hundred stations up and down the dial, but I found no news about a small-plane crash outside Lake Placid.

I rang the bell for the nurse, and when he appeared, I said, "I need my laptop. I need my phone. I need to speak with my family."

I listed my uncle and my brothers' names.

The nurse said, "You came in with the clothes you were wearing, dear. Nothing else."

"What's your name?" I asked him.

"Frankie. I'm on duty for another three hours."

Frankie handed me a glass of water and a paper cup of pills. I shook the little cup.

"What are these?" I asked.

"Pain pills, mostly."

"And what are the ones that aren't for pain?"

"Anti-inflammatory pills. You're running a little fever. And vitamins, of course. You need to rebuild your immune system…."

"Who makes these vitamins?" I asked.

The nurse looked at me blankly. "I get them from the pharmacy, already dispensed."

I flung the pills across the floor. I enjoyed the rattle and roll sound as they bounced off walls and chairs.

"I want to see my uncle Jacob."

Frankie scurried out of the room and I lay back, staring at the swirls of plaster in the ceiling. I thought about the plane crash, and snatches of the aftermath came to me.

I dimly heard the rhythmic whacking rotor blades of the helicopter dropping down on the hospital's helipad. Next, there were the sounds of wheels rolling under me, amplified voices through a PA system, and then hands lifting me from one bed to another.

A watery image came to me, the face of someone I'd seen through a gap in the curtain around my emergency room stall. The man had a short nose, honey-colored eyeglass frames, and hard little eyes. Uncle Pig. And I saw that he was talking to—Uncle Jacob.

Why had Peter been talking with Jacob?

More questions rose up from the bottom of my conscious mind. Why had our plane gone down? Why hadn't Jacob been with us? Had Sam's mother really died? Had there been a conspiracy? Had the whole airplane trip been cooked up so that all the Angels would die?

The single answer came to me as if I'd known it all along—and the horrible truth stunned me.

The crash had been no accident.

We were all supposed to die.

CONFESSION

Friend, I'm not afraid of death.

I'm not a religious person, and I've seen more than my share of dead bodies for a seventeen-year-old, including those of my parents. Thanks to my scientist father, I was raised with a healthy respect for the expiration date that we're all born with. We all have our moment in the sun, and it's what we do during our lives—not how or when we die—that makes up the interesting part of our obituaries.

But I refuse to go before my time.

I know I'm meant to do extraordinary things. Perhaps my personality has been shaped by the pills I've been taking my whole life, but I was never going to be a shrinking violet, drugs or not.

Here's a fairy tale for you. Once upon a time, I dreamed of a life where I went to an Ivy League college, then a Top Three business school, and eventually inherited the command of Angel Pharmaceuticals. I'd marry James, have a few kids, and live my life in fabulous luxury. It had all been perfectly mapped out.

Now I'm facing the very real possibility that I won't live to see my eighteenth birthday. Before that happens, I'm going to make sure that Angel Pharma—the company my father founded and hoped I'd helm one day—is completely destroyed.

Isn't it *crazy* how things change?

29

The light was pale blue in my hospital room. I found the call button, pressed it, and held it down until the door to my room opened and my nurse came in with Jacob behind him.

"Tandy, I'm here," my uncle said.

"Have you learned the cause of the crash?"

"Tandy, I haven't been home. I've been here with you and your brothers. The authorities will look into it. Everyone *lived*."

"It was a highly suspicious accident, wouldn't you agree?"

"You're understandably upset—"

"Have you forgotten the fire? Have you forgotten the

dead children in France, and that my brothers and I are a threat to Peter as long as we live?"

A doctor came into the room. He said, "I'm Dr. Reese. What's wrong here, Ms. Angel? Are you in pain?"

"I have to leave *now*."

He said, "Do you remember when we discussed taking something to calm you down?"

I'd never seen Dr. Reese before, ever, but I saw the needle coming toward me, and I began screaming, *"No, no, no!"* as I thrashed from side to side.

Alarms shrilled outside the door; the room filled with orderlies and nurses, and a gurney rolled into the room. Two people held me down, and I felt the prick of the needle in my hip.

I was lifted on the count of one-two-three. Jacob walked alongside me as we rolled down the corridor and into the elevator. I thought about Jacob talking with Peter.

What the hell was that?

I flailed and tried to climb off the gurney. I couldn't move except to open my mouth and howl. I screamed and clawed and twisted, and I cursed the men and women who loaded me into the ambulance.

I was still screaming when we pulled up to the emergency bay at Waterside.

30

The knockout drugs wore off pretty soon, a testament to how mad I was. And I mean mad as in *angry*, not *crazy*.

I was taken to a room that wasn't as nice as my old one. I didn't have a view of the highway and the river, but frankly, my friend, I didn't give a flying F about the view.

A nurse came in, one I knew quite well. Luann. She helped me into a long white cotton nightgown and snapped a plastic bracelet around my wrist with my name on it in capital letters.

She said, "Be right back," and when she returned, she had one little pill for me, not a cup of them.

"It's eight hundred milligrams of ibuprofen," she said,

handing me a cup of water. "Let's see you wash that right down."

I did it and got into bed.

I was in the white bed in the white room when Dr. Robosson arrived, wearing royal purple. She shrugged off her coat and sat down next to the bed, where I lay with hardly enough strength to get into a sitting position.

Without preamble she said, "I heard about the plane crash, Tandy. I think you've just overshot the amount of terror allowed by law."

"Look," I said. I pulled my nightgown up to my neck. My body was all bruises, especially vivid on my left side where I'd smashed into the armrest of my seat on the plane, but my neck, shoulders, breasts, both legs, and my left arm down to the wrist matched Dr. Robosson's coat, like they'd been colored by paint from the same pot.

"Jesus, Tandy," she said.

"Yeah. He was there, all right, or Uncle Peter would have had a very successful day's work."

"What do you mean?"

Dr. Robosson had a very, very, and I mean *very* concerned look on her face.

"I can't prove anything," I said. "But why, on a sunny day, in a new ten-million-dollar plane with a first-class pilot, did we have engine failure that should have taken out all four Angel kids at the same time?"

"What are you suggesting?"

I glared at her, like, *Come on. I have to spell this out?* Fine. I said, "Peter did it, Dr. Robosson. It totally fits him. And he had reason to want to get us out of the way."

"Tandy, how? How could Peter know Sam's mother had died? How could he have known that Matty would book a private plane? Even if he had known all of that, how could he have gotten to a mechanic to tamper with that aircraft in such a short period of time?"

I shrugged. I had been doped up for God only knows how long. Was I imagining things? Maybe I had never left Waterside. Maybe the last three weeks had been a dream.

"Let me ask you something," Dr. Robosson said. "Is it possible that because you had just seen Peter in court, and he won the case against you, your terribly traumatized mind made him the villain in this plane crash?"

"Let me ask *you*, Dr. Robosson. Do you think Peter Angel would let me live after I exposed his criminal activities in court, whether I won the case or lost? Do you think sabotaging an engine is impossible for him to do if he was determined to do it? Do you doubt he could tap phones, put fingers in pies or flies in ointments, and throw wrenches in the works if he wanted to?

"Because if you doubt that, you haven't been listening to me, Dr. Robosson. You've simply been placating me and wasting three full months of our lives."

"Of course I've been listening to you."

"You said I'm not paranoid," I said to her with all the power I could muster.

"You're not paranoid. But you're definitely a victim of too much brutality, both circumstantial and deliberate. I want you to rest, dear. You're very safe. Leo is outside now, watching the door. And he showed me his gun."

I smiled.

"I'll see you at lunchtime," said Dr. Robosson.

"Thanks, Mom."

Every time I called her Mom, I thought how much I wish my actual mom had been anything like her, anything at all.

I closed my eyes and tried to sleep.

31

Five days after I was admitted to the Waterside Center for Those Who Can't Cope or Don't Want To, Dr. Robosson released me back into the larger pool of misfits inhabiting New York City.

I couldn't *wait* to go home, but I also couldn't quite bring myself to call Leo. I wanted to walk for a bit and gather my thoughts in the crisp air.

Bundled up in my coat, scarf, hat, and boots, I walked east from Waterside in the morning light. I caught the downtown express at Dyckman Street, transferred to the local at 125th, and eventually came up for air on 72nd Street, just a few blocks south of the San Remo.

I was walking uptown on the sidewalk between the

looming apartment buildings on my left and the wide avenue of Central Park West, when a deep masculine voice called out, "Hey, Tandy!"

Who, me?

I looked up and saw that a black BMW was slowing as it approached. There were two men inside the car: the driver and a passenger, who seemed to be beckoning to me.

I was squinting into the sun, asking myself, "Do I know these men?" when a glint of sunlight hit something metallic in the passenger's hand.

I stopped moving. Every bit of me, including my brain, froze solid. That man was pointing a gun at me.

As sweat broke out over my entire body, the passenger took aim. I dropped to the sidewalk and rolled behind a parked car. I was hugging its rear tire when three sharp cracks rang out.

Yes, they were gunshots.

Jesus Christ. Someone was really trying to kill me. *Again.*

I felt cold, sick, and absolutely terrified, but I stayed balled up in a crouch as the BMW drove past. Then it was gone, but was I safe? Or was the shooter now walking up the street getting ready to take another shot at me?

I got out my backpack and dug around until I found my phone. I had to call 911.

But no. Not so fast, Tandy. My phone was dead.

What now?

I inched up from the sidewalk and looked around. I saw no black BMW, no man with a gun advancing on me. But I did see a yellow cab slowing to pick up a woman with a walker who was waving him down.

I jumped out of my hiding place and ran between this poor woman and the taxi. I may even have shoved her aside in my rush.

She yelled out, "Hey! That's mine!"

"Sorry," I said as I got in, pulled the door closed, and locked it.

I was shaking from the adrenaline overload, but I had to get it together. I shouted at the reflection of the driver's hard eyes in the rearview mirror.

"Twentieth Precinct. Eighty-Second between Amsterdam and Columbus. Floor it," I said. *"Fly."*

32

I was thrown against the backseat as the driver peeled away from the curb. He made a hard right and sped up Amsterdam.

Was this guy on speed? In a way, I hoped he was.

It was only a ten-block ride to the police station, but I had to call Jacob *now*. I grabbed the hand strap and put my mouth up to the holes in the Plexiglas divider separating me from the cabbie.

"Please, I need to use your phone."

"If I do that, miss, I'd have to let anyone use it."

"That makes no sense. I'll pay you for the call."

His eyes flashed to the rearview mirror. He looked angry. Definitely unstable. I probably looked that way, too.

He said, "I'll bet you not only have no phone, but no money, either."

"What did you say?"

He braked hard at a light, then turned to face me through the scarred plastic divider.

He said, "Show me your money. Or get out."

Was he insane? Yes. But I needed him.

I was panting, my heart going a hundred miles an hour. I shot him the dirtiest look possible, but I went through my wallet and pulled out my American Express Black Card.

"I need to use your phone," I said. *"Now."*

He passed his phone through the small door, and I called my uncle. No answer, so I left a message and held on to the armrests. Five minutes later, the cab stopped across the street from the brick and stone precinct house. I swiped my Amex through the card reader, left the bastard a generous tip, then sprang out of the cab.

I saw Caputo and Hayes halfway down the block, getting out of their squad car. I would recognize them from ten thousand feet away—in the dark.

Sergeant Capricorn Caputo is about six feet tall, stringy and dark-haired. His pants cuffs stop four inches above his ankles, and he has a vivid tattoo of a goat—his zodiac sign—on his left wrist. He's never in his life been called nice.

Detective Ryan Hayes is his partner's total opposite. He's stocky with thin brown hair, is a family man with kids, has no visible tattoos, and doesn't hide his soft side.

These were the cops who had come to our door when my parents had died. They were sharp, which I liked. But they had rushed to a faulty judgment that one or all the Angel kids had killed their own parents. That led to all-night interrogations, borderline harassment, and three of us being charged with murder and jailed.

Of course, the charges didn't stick.

No kidding. We hadn't done it.

After I solved the case, Caputo and Hayes knew I was solid. I worked other cases with them, solving those, too, and we had even become friends. Now I made my hands into a megaphone and called down West Eighty-Second Street, "Sergeant Caputo. Detective Hayes. It's Tandy...

"I need help!"

33

The squad room was tiny, crowded with four desks, four detectives, and no windows. I fixed my eyes and the force of my personality on Caputo and Hayes and said, "A man just fired three shots at me through a car window on Central Park West. It was a drive-by, but the shooter knew me. He called my name."

"So who was it that took shots at you, Tandy?" Hayes asked me. He looked worried.

"I don't know. But I have a pretty good idea who paid him to do it."

I quickly sketched in the horrific and humiliating recent events—the imploding lawsuit, the airplane crash, my history with my uncle, whom Caputo and Hayes had met.

"I have a lot of bad stuff on him, and—no lie—it all adds up to motive. It has to be Uncle Peter," I said. "He's tried to have me killed before."

"What happened exactly?" Hayes asked me as Caputo rooted around in his desk for a working pen. I told the detectives everything I knew about the shooter, which was pretty damned little: two seconds of staring at a car and a gun, and about ten seconds of hugging a tire.

"My take on it? He had to be a professional," I said.

Caputo said, "A pro? And he missed? You're not dead, right?"

"I ducked."

"And so he, what, figured out that you'd be on that block at that moment in time, and so he was ready to bump you off?"

"I don't know how he knew where I'd be."

"What kind of car?"

"BMW. A black sedan."

"Year?"

"I don't know."

"Plate number?"

"I wish. It happened too fast."

"The shooter. Was he white, black? Did he have facial hair?"

"White. I didn't see any facial hair."

Hayes asked, "Did anyone else see this drive-by?"

I said, "I was hiding behind a parked car."

Caputo stared at me, tapping his skeletal fingers on the desk as the other cops in the room talked loudly into their phones. How *had* that shooter known where to find me?

"Listen, Pansy, I don't know what you expect me to do. You can't identify the shooter, don't have a plate number, and there couldn't be more than fifty thousand BMWs in this city. Gimme a break."

"You *know* me. You know I don't make shit up."

Caputo sighed. "Candy, *if* the shots were fired and no one got hit and there're no witnesses, I've got nothing to go on and neither do you."

"Don't say *if*. It happened," I said, slapping Hayes's desk, hard. "So let's go to the scene and find the evidence. You can look for shell casings. Bullet holes. You can make this official. Besides, you owe me."

Hayes rubbed his chin and said, "Cap, we're not busy. We should do this for Tandy."

I beamed at Hayes.

"Thank you," I said. "Thanks very much."

34

Our sirens screamed as we sped down CPW toward the spot between Seventy-Third and Seventy-Fourth where I'd almost been shot.

The closer we got, the more anxious I became. I was starting to doubt myself. Had that shooting really happened? Had an unknown shooter really tried to kill me? How had he known how to find me? He could have tracked my phone using GPS, but my phone was dead.

I pointed out where I'd been walking when I saw the gunman. Caputo and Hayes gloved up and then unspooled yellow crime-scene tape, closing off the chunk of sidewalk I'd identified. They began to walk along the sidewalk. I saw them stop, stoop, and keep walking. Would they find pockmarks in the wall of the building, or maybe spent shells in the street, or bullet holes in a door or window?

And most importantly, would Caputo and Hayes find enough evidence to arrest my uncle Peter?

I watched Hayes talking to a doorman, and then my cop friends were stripping off their gloves, ripping down the tape, and stuffing it into a trash can.

Caputo came back to the car and, sneering, got in. Hayes confirmed what I had already guessed.

"We found no shell casings, no weapon, no evidence of any kind, Tandy. I'll file a report in case something turns up."

"You still have my number?" I asked him.

"I've got everything I need. We'll give you a lift home."

I said to Hayes, "Tell me you believe me."

"I believe you. But there's nothing to follow up. Do you understand, Tandy? We've done our best."

Why had there been no evidence of the shooting? Was this the right block? Had I gotten it wrong?

When we got to the entrance of the San Remo, I told Hayes I could take it from there. As the elevator rose to the sixteenth floor, I talked to myself.

I listed Peter Angel's crimes against me and my siblings, added up all the potentially deadly assaults that involved black cars and automatic weapons, house fires and knockout drugs, a kidnapping, having my memory wiped in a mental institution, a fatal car crash, a downed airplane, and about fifteen years of ingesting Angel Pharma drugs.

It was an outrageously long list, but I didn't feel sorry for myself. I was furious and trying to keep a lid on my emotions so that I could think logically.

I had no doubt that Peter was going to keep trying to kill me until he had done it. All evidence proved that he'd try to destroy my siblings, too. And with Katherine, he likely thought he'd succeeded.

The man kept trying and missing.

How long would it be before he got it right?

35

Jacob was waiting when I opened the front door. He was red-faced and clearly distraught, saying, "Tandy, my God. What happened? I got your message, but when I called back, I got someone who didn't know what the hell I was talking about or who you were. And he hung up on me. Did you say someone shot you? Are you hurt?"

I hugged my dear old uncle and then sang, "Lots of bad things keep happening, Uncle Jake. Lots of bad things. Lotta lotta lotta bad things. Lotta—"

"Shhh, Tandy, shhh. I've got you." He put his hands on my shoulders. "I'm here. You can count on me."

I felt the stress relax a bit and looked up at Jacob. "I'm sorry for scaring you and for not calling you back. My phone was dead. A man I don't know fired three shots at me," I said. "He missed. This time."

"Oh my God. Tell me everything," said Uncle Jake, walking me into the living room. Daylight was streaming through the windows from across the park, filling the apartment with a feeling of lightness and hope.

I didn't trust it.

I sat on the edge of the sofa, and Jacob took the chair. I told my uncle about the men in the car, my discussions with the cops, and how things had been left.

"No evidence. No case. Good-bye and good luck. Jacob, I'm a tough kid, right? I can take a lot. But no joke, I can't leave the apartment without a shitstorm raining down on me. Is this all for real or just my imagination?"

"I was at All Saints when you called," Jacob told me. "Oppenheimer asked me to come in."

"Okay," I said, asking myself, *What now?*

"He's suspending you for an indeterminate period, to be decided."

"What? Why?"

I was genuinely shocked. I had missed some time, but I could make it up. This term was just starting.

"He doesn't think you're well enough for school. He said you've missed a lot of days and that you were heard talking to yourself in class before the accident. He says you behave as if you're on drugs. That's what he said. Have you been using drugs, Tandy?"

Fury bloomed in my mind like a black flower.

"He thinks I'm on *drugs*?"

"You're not taking those pills again, are you, dear?"

"You cannot seriously be asking me that, Jacob. I sued to put Peter out of business over those pills and you ask me if I'm taking them?"

He looked at me with the question still on his face. The black flower in my mind was now full-blown. It blocked out the sun.

I snapped.

"Don't talk to me, okay? This is our apartment, not yours, so don't talk to me. Get it?"

Jacob snapped, too. "I'm your court-appointed guardian and your oldest living relative, Tandoori. When I speak, you will listen. And you will obey. Get *me*?"

I flew up to my room and slammed the door. I was hyperventilating and had that feeling you get when you know you've hurt someone but still feel you're right.

I felt trapped.

What the hell was I going to do now?

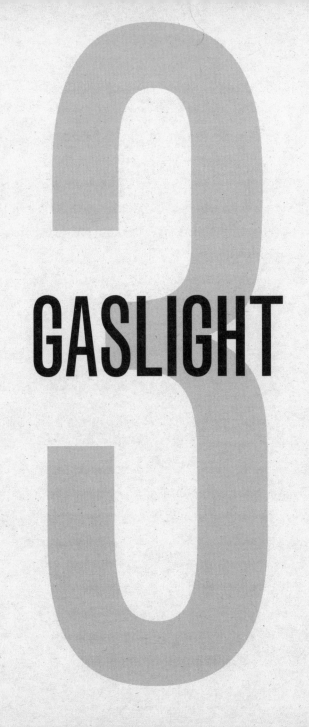

GASLIGHT

36

That night, Jacob and I exchanged tearful apologies, and over the following two weeks, my life quieted down. At least, it looked calm on the surface.

I didn't leave the apartment without the panicky feeling that someone would call my name and then gun me down. I could see this so clearly, it was as if it had already happened.

I took classes at home, Skyping with a witty college-girl tutor from NYU who had a keen knowledge of my high school subjects. I was luxuriating in my one-girl home-schooling program when C.P. started sending me spite mail. I got this one day: "James and I were just wondering, do you miss us, Tandoo?"

Seeing the name James in an e-mail from C.P. felt like an unknown assailant's bullet slamming into my rib cage and ricocheting around my chest cavity before ripping through my heart.

I wrote, "You need to stop obsessing over me, C.P. It's more than just a little pathetic." I changed my e-mail account *again*, then went outside my room and called down to Jacob.

"I need Leo to be my bodyguard tonight, okay?"

Later that day, I wriggled into a skintight black crepe dress with a low-cut asymmetrical neckline, heels high enough to make me look at least twenty, and Mom's wonderful spangled Madonna jacket. I slicked my hair back behind my ears and put on red lipstick and a pair of large black shades.

I looked like the very picture of *Vogue* Beverly Hills, eighties edition.

Hugo said, "You look hot. For you."

Hugo's broken nose was taped. He had two yellowish-black eyes, stitches in his upper lip, and a purple-green sunset of a bruise across his forehead.

I said, "You, on the other hand, look like you belong on *The Walking Dead*."

Hugo laughed out loud, which made the rest of us laugh, too. Once we were all inside the bulletproof car,

Leo drove Jacob, Hugo, and me to Carnegie Hall, one of the premier concert venues in the world.

Because Harrison Angel was playing tonight. My wonderful talented twin had the stage to himself.

Walking into the auditorium took my breath away with its grandeur. From the five-story-high tier of gold and red velvet seats that form an elongated semicircle to the glorious stage on which hundreds of eyes would be fixed all evening, the entire vast space is both a visual and an acoustic wonder.

Around us, people were talking about my brother. I heard one elegant lady saying to her husband, "This boy—he's something else, Bennett. I've been following him since his incredible debut in Paris. Prepare to have your shoes, socks, and jacket blown off. Hold on to your shirt and tie, too."

Concertgoers swirled around, finding their seats, the excitement on their faces making me so proud of my brother that my eyes welled up with tears—and he hadn't even taken the stage.

And then he did.

Wearing a tux, looking like the romantic hero in a Victorian novel with his dark curling hair and brooding eyes, my genius brother bowed at center stage. After a rolling tsunami of thunderous applause, he sat down at one of the two pianos on the stage, the Steinway grand.

I gripped Hugo's left hand and Jacob's right as the lights went down. There was an interminable silence as Harry sat on, his arms at his sides.

Whispers fluttered up to the ceiling like trapped birds, and I was suddenly afraid for Harry. Did he have stage fright? Was he having a panic attack?

For a moment, in the darkened hall, I thought I saw Katherine—and then Harry's hands jumped to the keys of the Steinway and he struck the opening notes in the concert he called "Acoustic Electric." His interpretation of "Black and White" by Reginald Trudeau resounded and filled the vast hall, and when I looked for my sister, I didn't see her at all.

But on the stage, Harry absolutely shone. After the first piece, he played three more in a series of four stunning compositions made famous by four pianists who had started out playing acoustic piano, only to move later to pickups, plugs, and amps.

The audience applauded their approval. I grinned at Jacob and shouted into his ear, "I can feel the vibrations through the soles of my shoes."

After intermission, Harry went to the electric piano and played a second piece by each of the four composers. Again the audience went crazy. Harry bowed deeply, then walked into the wings, and of course, the almost three thousand people packing Carnegie Hall demanded an encore.

I had thought the concert was over, but when Harry returned to the stage for another bow, I saw that he had a microphone in his hand.

He said into the sudden hush, "I want to close with a song I wrote for my sister Tandy. I call it 'We Will Always.'"

Sitting back down at the grand piano, Harry moved quickly into a catchy bossa nova tune. With its upbeat melody and distinctive beat, it surprised and delighted everyone.

I had wanted to be in disguise tonight. I wanted no attention at all, but I blushed as the whispers swelled and heads turned and people smiled, wiped away tears, and dipped their heads toward me as Harry played and sang his sweet and loving song about the two of us growing up together.

> *There's a place I remember,*
> *One my heart won't surrender.*
> *We could go there tomorrow.*
> *You could lead, I would follow.*
> *You've been with me for ages,*
> *Stumped the wits and the sages,*

Held my feet to the fire,
Raised my sights a bit higher.
We've known Paris in autumn.
We grew up in New York.
We recall the Dakota—
Everything that we lost.
I will never forsake you,
Force or remake you.
You've been one of a kind, dear.
You're my twin and my sister.
There's a place I remember,
Somewhere east of September.
We will someday return there,
We will always belong there.
There's a place I remember.
There's a place I remember.

37

At eleven thirty PM, *just after* Harry's concert, I boarded a Delta flight from New York's JFK Airport to Charles de Gaulle in Paris.

I never wanted to get on another airplane. Ever. But despite my stamping and pouting and the impressive, self-indulgent fit I threw, Jacob remained firm.

"Pack something nice to wear. Don't lose your passport. And try something new, why don't you? Trust me."

And now I was sitting in a window seat in first class with a glass of orange juice and a cup of warm nuts. I opened the note Jacob had slipped into my coat pocket curbside and read it again.

Tandy,

Life goes on. It just does, whether we're ready for the next chapter or not. Embrace it.

Love,
Uncle Jacob

I folded the note, placed it back into my pocket, and stared at the seat backs and the curtain drawn across the front of the cabin. The other passengers were asleep, but not me.

I would never forget the sickening sensation of gravity on a falling plane, knowing that I was about to die—and that the person responsible was going to get away with it.

Now, in the body of a big jet, I gripped the armrests so hard, I broke a nail. Peter wouldn't dare bring down a commercial airliner with hundreds of passengers just to get me out of his way. Would he?

I swear, I think he *would*.

That thought occupied me for hours. I sat upright, listening to air hissing through the vents and the snoring of the man in the seat beside me. I hummed "We Will Always" under my breath, and somewhere over the enormous Atlantic Ocean, I must have fallen asleep, because I was suddenly awakened by the bright sun in my window and an announcement. "Ladies and gentlemen, we will be landing shortly...."

I had traveled light, so I cleared customs quickly and emerged on the other side of the arrivals door to see a blond-haired man in livery holding up a sign with my name.

Georges greeted me in heavily accented English, took my bag from me, and led me out to the car. I asked him where he was taking me.

"The hotel is very nice, *mademoiselle*. At six this evening, a friend of yours will come to pick you up."

A friend of mine? Would it be my sister, Katherine?

"He is Monsieur Delavergne," said my driver.

Monsieur Delavergne is my deceased grandmother's head lawyer and director of her estate. What did this mean? Why was I meeting with Monsieur Delavergne?

I checked into Hôtel le Bristol on Rue du Faubourg Saint-Honoré, hung up my clothes, and slept as though I'd never been in a bed before. And sometime around six that evening, in the middle of the day according to my sleep cycle, Monsieur Delavergne rang up to my room.

"I'll be right down," I told him.

I'd been having a dream. I could still feel James's hands on me as we lay together in a small bed with moonlight coming through the window. We'd been looking into each other's eyes. He'd told me he loved me.

That bastard.

I showered and dressed in my new peaches-and-cream silk dress, which felt like clouds wafting around my legs. I stepped into a new pair of strappy pumps and finger-combed my hair. I slicked on some pale lip gloss and gave my eyelashes a hit of mascara.

Then I casually threw on a pale cashmere coat and scarf, softer than soft.

I checked myself out in the beveled pier glass.

I looked good. Actually, I looked my best. I snapped a selfie and texted my brothers:

This is me before my surprise evening with Monsieur Delavergne. What will happen next? ☺

I pressed send. I grabbed my room key.

Ready or not, a new chapter was beginning.

Showtime.

38

Short, balding, about sixty years old, with hair sprouting on his knuckles and creeping out of his shirtsleeves, Monsieur Delavergne is not gorgeous, and in my experience, not exactly fun, either. So I was surprised to see him behind the wheel of a shiny blue Mercedes-Benz in a sport jacket, pink linen shirt, no tie, loafers, no socks. And he was smiling at me.

"Tandy, are you feeling well?" he asked me in French.

I thought of all the possible answers to that one and decided to lie.

"*Bien*," I said. "*Je suis très bien.*"

He smiled.

He also looked very pleased with himself, and that was

good. The Angel kids really needed Monsieur Delavergne on our side. But as the car slowed to navigate the *très charmantes* winding streets of Paris's Le Marais district, I started to enjoy the lawyer's cheerful side. It felt like I was leaving the scary past behind.

When the car stopped in front of the powder-blue-and-gold building that housed the perfume company my grandmother had founded so many years ago, the attorney said, "This is a very big event. I'm pleased for you to be the flower of Parfumerie Bellaire. I hope you are ready for your close-up, yes?"

"What is it? What is happening?" I asked.

"It is your perfume," he said. "It is, how you say, rolling out today, worldwide."

My perfume?

Beautiful people in gorgeous clothes were spilling out from the store onto the adorable shop-lined street. There was a huge banner over the entrance to the shop that read INTRODUCING TANDOORI, THE SCENT OF LOVE.

I clapped my hands to my mouth. *This* was the reason I'd flown all this way. That a fragrance named for me was being introduced to the world, and this was the launch party. No wonder Monsieur Delavergne had been so lighthearted, pulling off such a stupendous treat.

But that was only the beginning.

The driver opened my door for me, and as the soles of my strappy shoes touched the street, a wonderful man who had loved my gram Hilda came out of the store, opened his arms, and embraced me. His name was Guillaume Laurier; he'd been with this company since my grandmother's time and had been the president for many years.

He had to be the one who had named a fragrance for me.

"You look beautiful," he said, kissing both my cheeks. He lifted two glasses of champagne from a tray, handed me one, and toasted me, saying, "To the original Tandoori."

I returned the toast. "I am so honored, Monsieur Laurier. I can only say, thank you so much."

"You wish to smell 'Tandoori, the scent of love'?"

"Oh, of course I do."

My silk skirts swirled around me as we parted the crowd and went into the shop. The walls were hung with huge, luminescent photos of flower fields in the French countryside: lavender and roses, and tall grasses backlit by the setting sun. There was a video playing on monitors: a gorgeous commercial for Tandoori.

Monsieur Laurier brought me to a table near the center of the store. A pinlight in the ceiling lit a rounded bottle of frosted glass with my name etched in the center.

My grandmother's old love lifted the bottle, tipped

it gently, righted it, and removed the stopper. Then he touched the stopper to the inside of my wrist.

All the people standing around us, the celebrities and the executives and the factory workers and the media, inhaled as one, their eyes filled with hope and sweet expectation.

I raised my wrist and let the scent of love come to me. It was floral and luxurious, spicy with striking notes of freesia, mandarin, bergamot, orange blossom, and orchid. It was simply delicious.

"How do you like it?" Monsieur Laurier asked me.

"*Parfait*," I said. "It is so absolutely perfect."

He took my hand and twirled me around as Monsieur Delavergne and all the other guests clapped their hands.

A man with a violin appeared and, unbelievably, played "We Will Always." My twin's song to me.

It *was* perfect.

But will it surprise you if I say that in that perfect moment, I couldn't help thinking of love lost?

I missed James.

CONFESSION

I was having a lucid dream.

I knew that I was dreaming and that I could control the whole story and even the ending—but I didn't want to change anything. I wanted the dream to spool out from my subconscious just as it was doing.

You see, I'd had this dream before.

In it, James and I were in bed together. Even though my eyes were closed, I saw him look at me in a special way. He reached out and touched my hair. Then he got out of bed and walked naked across the frayed carpet to the rickety old desk beside the armoire. There he wrote a note on a sheet of hotel stationery. I could read it as if I was standing behind him and looking over his shoulder.

Dear Tandy,

My father will seriously hurt you if he finds us together and I can't stand for that to happen. Don't ever think that I don't love you. I'm sorry.

James

In this dream, so much like the way it had actually happened, James dressed while standing in a fine beam of moonlight. Then he dropped the note onto the bedcovers, pulled on his leather bomber jacket, and left the room. The door closed behind him with a sharp clack.

When the door closed in my dream, I opened my eyes. I might have been able to manipulate the outcome of the dream: I could have made love to James, listened to him tell me he loved me over and over again.

But I preferred the truth…that James had firmly, decisively, closed the door.

39

I awoke in my huge bed on the top floor of the Hôtel le Bristol with its perfectly framed view of the City of Light. As I returned to the real world, I recognized the fragrance in the air as the perfume I had sprayed on my pillow last night.

Tandoori, the scent of love.

What a joke that was, linking my name to *love*.

To lift my despondent mood, I thought of Uncle Jacob. He had been emphatic: "Enjoy your time in Paris," he'd said. "Take it all in."

It was good advice. I needed a mental health break,

and I was in the haute couture capital of the world and in need of smart new clothes to make my nasty schoolmates jealous.

And I *would* be going back to school.

But first, shopping.

A few hours later, I was in a cab to Rue Montorgueil, a walking street lined with sidewalk cafés and shops in the Châtelet–Les Halles district in the center of Paris.

I paid my driver and had just stepped out onto the street when a woman's voice called my name.

This time I ducked first, *then* looked for the gun.

Meanwhile, my taxi zoomed off, leaving me exposed on all sides to the traffic whizzing past—and I heard her call me again.

"Tandy. It's *me*. It's Katherine."

I looked around. Was it really my sister? Or was this a trick? Then, through a break in the traffic, I saw her waving to me from across the street.

Oh my God, oh my God, oh my *God*. It was her. Katherine was wearing a blue shawl-collar wool coat and high boots. Her dark hair flowed over her shoulders, and sunlight limned her in a halo from shining head to polished toe.

She looked angelic.

I jumped up and down and waved, and she waved back, yelled my name again, and made her way to me. She dropped her bag to the street and hugged me hard.

"I love you, love you, love you so much," she said.

I said into her shoulder, "I love you so much, too, and, Kath, in the future, will you give me a heads-up, please? So I don't go into cardiac arrest every time you just appear."

She laughed. "Okay. If possible."

I'd last seen Katherine here, in Paris, and it had been absolutely heart-stopping to see her alive when I had long believed her to be dead.

She'd explained how she had survived the fiery accident that was no accident, but a deliberate attempt on her life. She revealed that she'd been rescued by a stranger who was hiding her in a mysterious location—secret even from me. She had told me then that we might never see each other again. It was much too dangerous, because of Uncle Peter.

But here she was.

Now, at this radiant, unexpected second meeting, Katherine said, "I went to your hotel, but I'd just missed you. Oh, I love your perfume. It must be Tandoori."

I said, "Good guess," and grinned like a fool. Then I

asked, "Kath, how did you know where I'm staying? How do you always know how to find me?"

"The less you know, the better, Tandy. Come. Let's walk. We shouldn't stand together in one place for too long."

40

I was strolling again with my wonderful big sister on a gorgeous avenue in this inimitable city, but instead of feeling content, I was watching everything and everybody, ready to scream, *"Gun!"*

We went to a bistro called Café du Centre at the end of the street. It's a wide-open restaurant with red awnings and lots of tables and chairs outside, with the best views of historic pastry, hardware, shoe repair, and tobacco shops.

"I saw Beyoncé here once." Kath laughed. "Really."

We took seats inside for privacy, and over cafés au lait and Niçoise salads, Kath showed me pictures of her little boy. He was adorable and looked so much like Kath, but

I couldn't get her to tell me about the baby's father, if she was married, or even what *continent* she called home.

She was saying, "When I heard about the launch of your perfume, I knew you would be there. I booked a flight, but it was delayed, dammit. Sorry I missed the party. Look at what I was going to wear," she said. She opened her bag wide and showed me a blond wig and big wraparound shades.

"You were going to go in disguise?"

"Nothing has changed, Tandoo. Be careful. Watch everything around you and maybe, one day..."

Just then, I saw a gray car, a Peugeot, speeding past the café. It cut off a blue Renault, and I watched the T-bone collision accompanied by the blare of car horns.

The cars were still rocking from the impact when Katherine's phone pinged. She glanced at it, then said to me, "Sorry. I have to take this."

She texted a message, read another, and typed a second text, then apologized again and called for the check.

"I have to go right now," she said. "I love you, T."

I said, "Kath, are you serious? What's wrong? I can't believe you're leaving already."

Katherine said nothing.

She kissed me on both cheeks, then held my head with her cheek pressed to mine as if she was saying good-bye forever. When she released me, she put money down on the table, then fled. Baffled, I watched her run directly toward the dusty gray Peugeot that had caused the accident. By now it had backed away from the other car and was readying to take off in the opposite direction. I couldn't make out who was driving.

I was out of my chair, knocking into the waiter as I ran after my sister. I called to her from the doorway.

"Katherine, *wait*! I'll come with you!"

She waved and blew me a kiss before getting into the passenger seat of the Peugeot and closing the door. And then my beautiful, mysterious sister was gone. Again.

41

That night, I sat by myself in the first-class lounge with my new, oversized Gerard Darel handbag, *Marie Claire Paris*, and a glass of Perrier, waiting for my flight to be called.

I wasn't actually reading the magazine. I was replaying my meeting with Katherine. Having felt for a short while that we were closer than ever before, I now began to question all of it.

How *had* Katherine found me after I had left the hotel? I hadn't told anyone where I was going. Who was driving the gray Peugeot? Why had he caused that crash? Had that driver and my sister been following me? They must have been—but why?

These thoughts circled in an endless loop as I sat alone in the timeless vacuum of the flight lounge. Then my thoughts were derailed by an incoming phone call from Monsieur Delavergne.

I picked up.

"Tandy, I am sorry I didn't say good-bye in person."

"No worries, Monsieur Delavergne. Thanks for sending a car."

"You're welcome, *mademoiselle*. Also, I wanted to confide something to you."

He had every bit of my attention. The only sound in the world was Monsieur Delavergne's voice in my ear.

"What is it, Monsieur Delavergne? What's wrong?"

"It's about Jacob," he said.

"What about him?" I gripped the phone so tightly that I snapped a photo of my knees and almost disconnected the call. "Monsieur Delavergne? Can you hear me?"

"I am still here, Tandy," he said in French.

And just then my flight was announced right over my head. I asked Monsieur Delavergne to wait for the announcement to end, and when I finally had reestablished a cone of silence, I asked him again, "What *about* Jacob?"

"It is not going so well for him," Monsieur Delavergne said. "Just watch him. And if you need to call me, I am always here for you."

"Be more specific," I said. "*Please*. What should I look for? What's wrong with him?"

But Monsieur Delavergne was saying, "Have a safe flight. It was good seeing you again, Tandoori. Be kind."

Be *kind*?

"*Au revoir, ma chérie.*"

"*Au revoir*," I responded, to a dead phone line.

I went to the gate and boarded my flight to New York. Then I went into my head for the next eight hours, wondering what the hell Monsieur Delavergne had been hinting at.

Add to that my plane-crash paranoia, which had me jumping at every hum, rattle, hiss, and captain's announcement. In between hyperlistening, I prayed that the plane would stay aloft until it landed smoothly on the runway in New York.

I couldn't eat or read or sleep. Instead, I watched a movie without the sound while I pondered the imponderable.

How had Katherine found me? Why had she left in such a rush?

Why was everything about Katherine so mysterious?

42

The next morning, Jacob was making hot cocoa when I trundled wearily into the kitchen.

"Welcome home," he said. "Come in and pull up a chair, Tandy. I want to hear all about your trip in actual words, not bloody texts."

"Pictures, too, right?"

"You bet."

The kitchen in our new home was airy and modern. Jacob poured hot cocoa into mugs and placed a platter of just-baked cookies on the long metal table. I thanked him. Actually, I totally needed the warmth and the sugar.

"Start talking," Jacob said when we were both sitting down. "Don't leave anything out."

I'd been wide-awake since leaving Paris, wondering about Monsieur Delavergne's oddly veiled warning, but I kept that part to myself and gave Jacob some highly animated highlights of the Tandoori launch party.

"Monsieur Delavergne is nicer than I thought," I told Jacob, showing him a selfie of me with the lawyer in the pink linen shirt, photo-bombed by a cute woman spraying perfume over our heads.

Jacob grinned. "That's a keeper."

"And I saw Katherine," I said, scrutinizing Jacob's face, looking for any cracks in his affect that should worry me. I saw nothing.

I swiped my phone and showed him pics of the two of us in the bistro. "We were just having the greatest time, and then there was a deliberate car crash on the street. A second later, Katherine got a text, said, 'I've gotta go,' and then ran outside, got into one of those cars—and *poof*! She was gone."

"Tandy, was she scared? Or what did you make of that?"

I shrugged. "It seemed like her ride called her and she had to go. Another mystery," I said. "And how have you been, Uncle Jake?"

"Me? Same as always. Harry stayed home from school for a couple of days, recuperating, catching up on his mail, and so on. Hugo has been steady. I haven't heard from Matthew."

"How are *you*?" I insisted.

"What are you getting at, Tandy? I take care of things. That's my job. Are you done with your cocoa?"

He took away the mug and I told him I'd be in my room. I unpacked the bags I hadn't wanted to deal with earlier and charged up my electronics and then sat at my desk and watched the sky darken above the park. I thought about Jacob. I couldn't even guess at what he might be hiding, but he was definitely holding something back.

Why would he hide anything from me? I considered this question through my new, highly focused lens of paranoia.

Jacob had been in France the day my brothers and I took Peter to court. If he had been with us, he would have lent credibility to our case. Jacob knew that Angel Pharma pills had killed people.

Another thing—Jacob hadn't been with us when our plane crashed on the way to Lake Placid. But *after* the crash, while I was in the emergency room, I'd seen Jacob speaking with Peter.

And that led me to a long-standing mystery that had never been answered to my satisfaction. Why had Peter turned over the guardianship of the Angel kids to Jacob, an uncle we had never even known existed before our parents' deaths?

Was Jacob even our uncle at all?

I was nearly overwhelmed with confusion—and I didn't like that one bit. I flashed on the hundreds of pills I had emptied out onto the conference table at Peter's lawyer's office. I had more pills stashed in the apartment.

If only I could sedate myself with a handful of Num.

Who could blame me for wanting the clarity of a crisp, emotionless state? How else could I know up from down in my Alice-in-Horrorland existence? Was what I believed to be my life history in any way real? Or was it all a dream?

If so, whose dream was it?

And who was I? That was the question.

Did anyone know the answer?

43

I awoke out of a dreamless black hole of sleep to find myself staring at a star field of sleet coming straight at me, stinging my cheeks. A wet wind was blowing hard at the skirt of my nightgown; my arms were stretched out like wings in flight.

It took a second to understand, to really *get* that this was no dream.

I was standing outside on the ledge of the living room terrace with the railing *behind* me, my toes curled over the wet, slippery edge, *sixteen stories above the street*.

I screamed and beat at the air as I started to teeter. This could *not* be happening—but it *was*.

I made a backward grab for the railing behind me and

caught it, tightening my cold hands around the wrought iron, holding on tight even as my legs shook and wobbled.

What had happened? How had I gotten out here?

Have I gone crazy?

I had no memory of unlocking the French doors, crossing the terrace, and climbing over the railing, let alone making my way downstairs. I couldn't conceive of deliberately going out to the gritty edge of the building like it was a diving board.

But this was not a hallucination or a dream…no trick of an overactive mind. Two hundred feet below me, cars sped through the slush on the avenue.

If I fell, I would make a snow angel like no other.

Screw *that*.

I had to get off this ledge, and there was no room for error. If I sneezed or panicked or lost my awkward backhanded grip, I wouldn't get a second chance. I was going numb, quaking with terror, when a sober, instructive voice inside my head said, "Turn around, Tandy. Take your time."

With precise attention to where I placed my frozen toes and how I reversed the grip of my rigid fingers, I turned little by little, finger over finger, until I was facing away from the street, holding the railing tightly with both hands.

I wasn't safe yet. I still had to climb over the railing and onto the terrace. From there, I could get to a door or a window.

Just then, as I carefully began to haul my numb and shaking limbs over the rail, things went from horrific to hellish. As if I'd been punched in the gut, I was hit with stomach cramps. I fought back the pain and nausea and pulled myself up and over the railing. As soon as my weight was over the terrace, I let go of the railing and collapsed in a heap, retching helplessly in the snow.

I lay there, sick and panting from fear and exhaustion. *What was happening to me?*

Was I overdosing? But I hadn't taken any drugs. Had I?

I heard glass shattering several yards away; then Hugo's face poked out through a broken window. "Tandy, what's wrong?" he cried.

I gathered myself and rolled up onto my hands and knees. Hugo was there beside me, trying to help me stand, but my legs wouldn't hold me.

I saw blood streaking my nightgown. Panicking, I realized it was streaming from his wrist.

I screamed, "Hugo, you're hurt! Go get Jacob...*now*!"

44

I pulled myself to my feet using a deck chair as a crutch. I was still trying to get my balance when Harry came flying through the terrace doors and ran over to me.

Jesus, he was scared. I could hardly look at him because I didn't know what the hell to say.

He grabbed my arm and shook it until I looked at him. "Are you hurt? What happened to you?"

"I'm freezing," I said.

"Okay, okay, I've got you."

He put my arm over his shoulder and walked me carefully through the mushy snow on the terrace, through the French doors, and into the living room.

My lips were frozen and my voice shook as I said, "Harry, Hugo is bleeding."

And then Jacob was there in front of us, absolute shock and horror on his face. He looked at me, at the blood on my nightgown, and I knew he thought I'd attempted suicide.

That wasn't true. Was it?

I said, "Jacob. Hugo cut himself badly on the window glass. Please see to him."

At any other time, Jacob would have said, "It's going to be okay. I'm here."

But he said, "Tandy. Take a hot shower. Then call Dr. Robosson's service. Say it's an emergency and make an appointment for first thing tomorrow morning. If you don't do it, I will take you there myself."

I nodded numbly and headed for the stairs.

Jacob was right to think I had lost my mind. If I didn't get help, I didn't know how I was going to get it back. As I climbed the spiral staircase, I watched Jacob wash Hugo's arm in the kitchen sink. Blood ran down the drain, and Hugo screamed when the peroxide followed the soapy water.

"Does he need stitches?" Harry asked.

"I don't think so," said Jacob. "The cut is shallow. More like a scratch, right, young man?"

This was my fault.

What the hell was wrong with me?

45

It was Saturday, the day after I had almost flown off the sixteenth-floor balcony. I had just come home from my emergency session with Dr. Robosson, who had explained that my nocturnal and unconscious trip to the ledge was sleepwalking, possibly caused by so much stress.

If she was right, it was the first time I had ever walked in my sleep. But I had no better explanation.

Before I had been discharged from Waterside, Dr. Robosson had given me a prescription for sleep meds and a few samples, which I had in my backpack. I hadn't taken one of those samples, had I? Dr. Robosson and everyone else knew I was against pills. *All* pills.

But I had a plan...what to do for everyone's safety

and peace of mind. It was a sickening plan, but it was necessary.

I called Uncle Peter from the sanctuary of my pretty blue bedroom. "We need to talk."

"Go ahead," he answered.

"I want to talk to you in person."

"Do you wish to meet under the clock in Grand Central? I'll wear a carnation in my lapel. Pink."

"That won't be necessary," I said. "I'll come to you."

I still saw it as my life's mission to put Angel Pharma out of business, but I wanted to buy a little time to live without fearing the sound of my name. I needed to think, to plan, rather than react. To gather myself. And I was willing to humble myself and promise anything to get Peter to give me and my brothers some space.

I made sure my phone was charged and that I had Jacob, Leo, Harry, and the Twentieth Precinct all on my speed dial. I dressed modestly in dark trousers and a turtleneck for my meeting with my would-be assassin. Then I called Leo and asked him to bring the car around.

I had only been to Peter's apartment once.

I had been in the fourth grade, and he had invited all of us to dinner. Katherine was still with us then, and as usual, all of Peter's attention was on her. He seated her in the chair next to his at the table. He gave her a gilded book on Catherine the Great and asked her opinion on all manner of things. He was really, really nice to her.

At fifteen, Katherine was already a mathematical prodigy and a superb athlete, and she was becoming a real beauty. Peter asked her if she would like to go to Europe with him that summer, and my parents seemed to think it was a wonderful opportunity.

Why hadn't they seen Peter for the monster he was?

I now knew that this was the summer when Katherine had gone to France. I knew from Jacob that Peter had used my sister as a lure, a recruitment tool to persuade parents to sign up their children as guinea pigs for Angel Pharma.

Jacob had introduced me to one of those sets of parents when I was in Paris last fall. I had seen pictures of their triplet sons who had taken the pills and had died before they reached their twentieth birthdays.

Was what happened to those children happening to me and my brothers and sister now?

Leo pulled up to the Smithfield, an apartment building at Eighty-First and Columbus, close enough to our home on the West Side of Manhattan. The doorman rang up to Peter's apartment, and I heard my uncle's voice over the intercom.

"Send her up."

I was afraid of what was about to happen. Would Peter

hear me out? Would I lose my nerve? I pushed the elevator button, then clasped my shaking hands.

The elevator took me to the tenth floor, and the doors opened. I looked in both directions and saw that an apartment door had been left ajar at the far end of the hallway. It gave the appearance of a trap.

I shook out my hands and thought of Leo circling the block in the car. If I didn't call him in a reasonable amount of time, he would come upstairs looking for me.

I walked down the long carpeted hallway to the half-open door. It swung open on soundless, well-oiled hinges. I peered into the foyer and called out, "Uncle Peter?"

His voice came to me from the depths of his apartment.

"Come on in, Tandoori. I'm here."

Said the spider to the fly.

46

I found Peter sitting in front of a drafting table at one end of the room. He was working at a sleek computer but looked up when I came in and said, "Be with you in a minute. Have a seat."

He pointed to the other side of the room, which was furnished with two red upholstered office chairs, a square metal table between them. There were no paintings on the walls, no clue to the nature or interests or personality of the man who lived here, no signs that Peter Angel was the devil incarnate. Which he was.

As directed, I took a seat.

While my uncle finished what he was typing, I took in the closed doors and wondered what they led to. I smelled a faint fragrance that I almost recognized. And I noticed two cups and saucers on a tray on the kitchen counter.

Finally, Peter pushed back his chair, then came over and sat down next to me. He stared at me through his thick glasses with the butterscotch-colored frames, which matched his messy ginger hair.

He said, "What do you want, Tandoori?"

I stammered as I tried to get out my rehearsed request, finally managing it.

"I want to call a truce, Uncle Peter."

"Spell it out," he said.

"Okay. I will stop invoking your name as an enemy. I will not look for legal redress for any crimes you may have committed against me and my brothers, nor will I testify against you if I'm ever asked to. I will put that in writing. All I want in exchange is for you to leave us alone. I especially want Hugo to grow up in complete safety."

Peter sat back in his chair and shook his head.

Was he turning me down? Was he actually saying no to my proposal?

I think I saw smoke coming out of his mouth when at last he said, "I am a ruthless businessman. I'm proud of that. Would I destroy you if you got in my way? Of course. But I'm not a murderer. I would never try to kill you, and I never have. Any other questions?"

"So we have a deal?" I said in a squeaking voice.

"We don't *need* a deal," he said. "Now get out."

Now get out was more than a slap across the face. It was like a crowbar to the side of my head. Emotionally, I reeled. I realized that I had actually expected him to shake my hand, to lay down arms, to agree to agree.

Jamming my trembling hands into my pockets, I left my uncle's apartment knowing that nothing had changed. Whatever he planned to do to me—to *us*—there was nothing I could do to stop him.

I had stood up to Peter with all my drive, ingenuity, and determination, and I'd even come begging. Nothing had worked.

I had never felt so completely powerless in my life.

Leo was waiting for me outside the Smithfield. He opened the car door, and I got in. As we pulled out into traffic, he looked back at me through the mirror. He must have read the total defeat in my face.

"Is there anything I can do for you, Tandy?"

Leo's hat was lying on the seat beside him, so I was looking at the lifeless eyes tattooed on the back of his scalp.

For the first time, I asked myself if Leo was who he seemed to be.

He worked for us, but Jacob had hired him and Jacob

paid his salary. Supposedly. Or did Leo work for Peter, the mastermind of the plan to wipe out our family?

Was pistol-packing Leo one of Peter's plants?

Now, *that* was crazy. Right?

"Thank you, Leo. There's nothing you can do."

There was nothing anyone could do.

47

That evening, we had takeout from Curry in a Hurry. Everyone seemed preoccupied and moody, but at least we were together. After tidying up, I went to my room, shut off the lights, and covered myself with blankets to my chin. I needed sleep, badly.

But I hardly got any.

I was ripped out of sleep by a shocking, agonizing pain in my abdomen. My eyelids flashed open, and I instantly got my bearings. I was in my bed, for sure.

But I was very over-the-top sick to my stomach.

I balled up my pillows, held them tight against my belly, and curled around them, but that didn't help. It was just past midnight. Jacob would still be awake.

Groaning, almost doubled over, I hobbled along the hall to Jacob's door and fell against it. I knocked weakly and called him. He appeared almost instantly in his doorway, wearing shorts and a T-shirt and a fearful, almost angry look on his face.

I'm sure he was thinking, *What the hell is it now?* Honestly, I don't know how he can stand me.

"What's wrong, Tandy?"

"I'm very sick, Jacob. The pain is—oh my God—*excruciating.* I think I've been poisoned."

My knees buckled, and I collapsed at his feet, rolled into a fetal curl. He stooped down and put his hand on my forehead. Right after that, I heard him calling for help, waking up my brothers. I felt like a jerk, but I couldn't do anything to help myself. I couldn't even sit up.

Jacob and Harry wrestled me into a pullover and a pair of corduroy pants right over my pajamas. Hugo worked on getting socks and boots on my feet.

And that was when I lost it. I heaved, and a wastebasket somehow appeared under my chin. I used it, but instead of feeling relief, I felt worse, and now a rubber hammer had begun banging inside my head.

I must have blacked out, because the next thing I remember is a pair of EMTs lifting me onto a stretcher. There was a long trip through the lobby, radios crackling in my ears and my twin's reassuring voice saying, "We're with you, Tandy. We're right here."

The temperature outside was twenty degrees, but I was sweating like it was high noon in the Amazon rain forest. Jacob sat with me in the ambulance while I writhed and twisted and moaned.

He said, "We're almost there, Tandy. Hang on."

I grunted and managed to say, "I saw Peter today."

"Really?" Jacob said. He didn't believe me, but I needed to confess.

"I waved the white flag, Jacob. Total surrender. *Owwwwww!*" I yelped, grabbing my belly. "My God, this really hurts."

I fought through the pain and kept talking.

"I told Peter I wouldn't bother him anymore. Just to leave us alone. He didn't go for it. I'm sorry, Jacob."

"Don't be sorry. You'll feel better as soon as the doctors see you."

"I've doubted you, too."

"What do you mean?"

"I've questioned you because too many bad things have happened since you came to live with us. I've been thinking you—*Oh, this hurts so much.*"

Jacob took my hand.

"Rest, Tandy, please just rest," he said.

"No, I have to say this. Please forgive me, Jacob. I thought you could be working with Peter. His inside man."

"That's the pain talking," Jacob said. "You're really sick, Tandy. I don't know for how long, but you've been suffering from one thing or another since I met you."

"Do you think I'm crazy?" I asked him.

Tears leaked out of the corners of my eyes.

"Define *crazy*," he said.

I laughed one short *ha*. For a second or two, I felt good. Jacob wasn't mad at me, but the memory of all my suspicions about him came back with the pain.

The emergency room was packed with the sick and sicker. When someone got to me, my stomach was pumped, my blood was pulled, and I was sponge-bathed by a nurse with a very rough hand.

After checking my chart, the emergency doctor said, "Looks like you had food poisoning. Did you eat something in the last few hours that the other members of your family didn't eat?"

I thought about dinner. I pictured the table and the dishes we had ordered. And I remembered.

"We had Indian takeout. I had the tandoori prawns," I said. "Everyone else had curry. Lamb. Beef."

"Yep, seafood will do it. You feel a little better now?"

"When can I go home?"

"I want you to spend the night here. Let's see how you're feeling in the morning," said the doctor. "The nurse will give you something to help you rest."

I took the pills without protest and collapsed into a deep, troubled sleep.

48

Dr. Robosson was highly concerned. "Tell me what's hurting you," she said.

"Physically?"

"Emotionally."

"I don't know where to start. And please don't tell me to start at the beginning. I don't think I know what the beginning is."

"Tandy, start wherever you want to."

"I think I could die soon, Dr. Robosson."

"Are you suicidal?"

"Not in the least," I said. "I'm fighting off every attack. You know that."

"Then you're not going to die."

"I thought you wanted me to talk."

"I do. I'm sorry. Go ahead," said my shrink, leaning back in her brown velvet recliner.

I took some long breaths in and out. I spoke to myself inside my head about how I really liked Dr. Robosson but thought there was a good chance she wasn't enough shrink for me. I was too odd a case. Too smart, too damaged— physically, mentally, and psychologically. And I was a target. I had to tell her all of this.

Confession time.

"Don't take this the wrong way," I said. "I'm sick on too many fronts for one doctor to handle, even you. The damage was done long before I met you. And when I say I could die, I'm not being dramatic. Many attempts have been made on my life."

"Go on," she said.

"My uncle Peter wants me dead. He is crafty and rich and doesn't want to get actual blood on his hands. But I believe he has paid some people I count as friends to watch me and to report back to him. I believe that he has hit men at his disposal."

"Your uncle wants to kill you."

"Yes."

"So, please indulge me, sweetheart. Do you think he caused that airplane to go down?"

"There's a very strong possibility. It would have saved him a lot of trouble if my brothers and I had all died at the same time."

"And the drive-by shooting?"

"I would say a definite yes to hired gun."

"And the sleepwalking?"

"I looked up sleepwalking. It's caused by 'uninhibited REM' or 'sleep behavior disorder.' Stress contributes to that."

"Correct," said Dr. Robosson.

"Now, did Peter stress me out? Absolutely. Did he give me food poisoning? I don't know. Let's say he didn't do that. But there are too many other things that I can point to, Dr. Robosson—kidnapping and gunmen and fires— that just cannot be accidents."

She didn't protest. I saw love and concern in her face.

I said, "I need someone I can trust to know that if I die, it's murder, so that my uncle won't get away with it."

"Do you trust *me*, Tandy?"

I had to think about it. "Yes."

"Then here's what I need you to do."

49

I went directly from Dr. Robosson's cream-colored office to the high-tech lab on the floor above it. My blood was drawn for the second time in two days—six big vials of it this time—and I also had a CT scan of my brain.

After all that, I was taken to a pleasant white room with a big electric clock on the wall and a clean pine desk upon which were a stack of paper and a lot of pens. I started working on a battery of psychological and neurological tests, similar to ones I had taken before.

Usually, a person takes these tests over four nonsequential days.

I did them all in six hours.

After setting down my pen, I was escorted back to

Dr. Robosson's office, and I took my seat opposite her in her big brown recliner. I could see through the window behind her. Wet snow fell and stuck to the leafless branches.

"Tandy. How are you feeling right now?"

"Do you have the test results?" I asked her.

"I do."

"I'm ready."

She had a couple of papers on a clipboard on her lap, but she didn't look at them.

She said, "Your cortisol is through the roof. That's a result of stress. Otherwise, your blood work is normal. Your CT scan is the same as when you came here for the first time. You have no tumors, no aneurysms, no brain damage.

"Intellectually, you are off the charts," she said. "High genius, as you know. Very high. Psychologically, you have severe trust issues and fears of many things. Given your history, I don't find these fears psychotic."

"So I tested normal, right?"

"Well, normal for someone who has seen active duty in a war zone."

"Okay."

"I'm prescribing antianxiety medication and something for your uninhibited REM sleep disorder. We have to monitor your reactions to these meds and perhaps make adjustments."

"You know how I feel about 'medication,'" I said, making air quotes around the last word.

"I understand," said Dr. Robosson. "The meds are not permanent, but you need help now in order to go back to school and function in daily life. They can give you some relief from stress until your life normalizes, and it will. And you definitely need to sleep."

"Thanks, Mom. Please don't forget what I've told you."

"I won't," she said.

Dr. Robosson wrote out the scrips, set up another appointment for us later in the week, and gave me a big hug.

The snowstorm had turned the sky dark, and everything else was pretty much a whiteout.

Leo drove slowly and carefully to a twenty-four-hour pharmacy, where I picked up my thirty-day supply of pills, and then he took me home.

We had a late dinner of comfort foods: mac and cheese, creamed spinach, chocolate pudding with whipped cream. Nothing hard, crunchy, chewy, or spicy. It was a pretty tame family dinner—for us.

The first chance I got, my friend, I flushed the drugs down the toilet.

CONFESSION

Can't sleep. My mind is racing.

I'm thinking of the Angel pills, and how I would've solved this case by now if I was still taking them. Just one little Lazr, and my focus would be unmatched. Uncle Peter would be behind bars by now.

Would it be worth it, just to see that happen?

Just this one time?

50

The next morning, Leo parked our car outside Matty's apartment in Tribeca. He started to get out, but I stopped him, saying, "Wait here, Leo. I'll go."

"The snow is deep and slippery," Leo said.

"Not a problem. Really."

I opened my door and stepped knee-deep into the slush at the curb. Icy water spilled in over the tops of my boots, but I didn't flinch.

I crossed to Matty's building, rang his bell, and entered at the buzz. There was an arrhythmic thump and drag of his footsteps inside his apartment, and then my brother flung open the door.

"I want to talk to you privately," I said.

"Good morning to you, too, Tandoo."

He cracked a big smile.

He was wearing jeans, one leg of them cut off at the thigh to accommodate his broken leg; he also had on a beautiful white shirt, a silk tie, and a nice blue jacket. He looked *great*.

"Don't say anything personal in front of Leo," I said. "I just don't trust him, okay? Where's your coat?"

I helped Matty on with his overcoat and filled him in briefly on the drive-by shooting as well as my sleepwalking and food poisoning incidents.

"Christ, Tandy. You need an exorcism," he said.

"Ha. Exorcism for an Angel. Perfect."

Leo helped Matty into the backseat of the car, then drove us uptown to an office building on Third Avenue where Gram Hilda's estate lawyers had rented a conference room for the sole purpose of meeting with Matty.

I think we both knew what was coming: a strong admonition, a heartfelt apology from Matty, and then a check.

I entered the room with my arm around Matty's waist. Monsieur Delavergne greeted me with a smile, but he was once again in his professional role. He reintroduced us to the four lawyers accompanying him, but clearly, as before in Paris, it was Monsieur Delavergne's meeting.

When we were seated, Monsieur Delavergne addressed Matthew.

"Mr. Angel," he said in his accented English, "I understand the gravity and the impact of our decision on you, and that is why we have made this trip."

Matty nodded his big head and said, "Thanks for giving me a chance to speak for myself."

"Eh, actually, that won't be necessary," said the head lawyer. "The committee has met to discuss the terms of your inheritance and unanimously agreed that you violated the one condition of your trust fund. I am referring to the drunk-driving incident involving property damage and underage female passengers. This disgraceful occurrence reflects badly on the family name. But you know this.

"I'm very sorry, but you left us no choice but to terminate your inheritance."

"What do you mean *unanimously*?" Matty asked. I felt his body tense up. "You met with my uncle Jacob. I'm sure he voted *against* this decision."

"As I said, the decision was unanimous," said Monsieur Delavergne. "We are sorry, but we have to follow the dictates of the trust. We all wish you well."

"Like hell you do," Matty roared. "I have bills. I can't play football. People are suing me."

"I'm sorry," Monsieur Delavergne said again.

"Not sorry enough," my brother bellowed, rising to his full six-foot-two-inch height. Even with one of his legs encased in plaster, Matthew Angel had strength and balance to spare.

I watched in shock as Matty picked up his chair, raised it over his head, and threw it toward the windows. After the chair bounced off the reinforced glass, it knocked over a gigantic coffee urn, and china cups flew off the credenza.

Before the crashing subsided, Matty pushed me aside with one arm, then flipped the conference table. The lawyers scrambled to their feet and just barely got out of the way as the table upended.

Matthew was out of control, and it was worse than scary. What would he do next? What did the *pills* make him capable of doing?

Matthew looked at each of the lawyers in turn with his laserlike blue-eyed stare. I'd seen him steamroll professional football players many times. He'd broken ribs and shattered femurs. What else could he do?

Was he capable now of murder?

I was yelling his name, telling him to calm down.

He said, "I *am* calm, Tandy."

Then he blew out of the conference room like a hurricane on a crutch. The meeting about Matty's inheritance was officially over.

Matthew was *done*.

51

I left a devastated Matty in Charlie's Tap Room on Mott Street and arrived home at three that afternoon. I was in a black and violent mood, and for that I blamed Uncle Jake.

My poor brother.

How could Jacob have gone against Matty, siding with Gram Hilda's callous board when Matty was so down and so out?

I dropped my bag in the foyer and went looking for my uncle. I found him at his desk in his bedroom, talking on the phone.

I said, and not too nicely, "We have to talk."

He held up his index finger, the universal signal for *I'll be with you in a minute.*

"We need to talk right *now*," I said.

"Hold on, Peter," he said into the phone. "Tandy, please leave and close my door as you make your dramatic exit."

This was my Israeli former commando uncle speaking: a killer with lethal, registered hands. When he gave an order, you had to obey.

But you didn't have to like it.

I shot him one of my filthiest looks and left his room, slamming the door, then put my ear to the wood. I heard Jacob throw the lock, then continue conversing with Peter, pausing for Peter to speak and then speaking again himself.

I could only make out one word. *Tandy.*

Then I heard Jacob say, "Okay. Later."

I stood at the door like a freaking sentry outside Buckingham Palace. I waited. I heard drawers open and close. And finally, when I was about to kick the door down, it opened.

Jacob jumped back.

"For God's sake, Tandy."

"What you did to Matthew was really dirty, Jacob."

"You obviously don't know what you're talking about."

"No? While we were in court facing off with Peter, while we were flying in a sabotaged airplane, you were supposedly in Paris fighting for Matty to retain his inheritance."

"I *was* in Paris," Jacob said. "I went to the meeting. My input was requested and then, after listening to the others, I voted with the board."

"You were supposed to *fight*."

"I'm on the board, Tandy. It's a responsibility. Matty violated the terms of the trust. I didn't call for punitive action, but I don't disagree with the decision to withhold his inheritance.

"If I start blindly throwing my vote to you kids, then I'll have no credibility and maybe no seat at the table, either. And I can almost guarantee that in the next forty years, you will *want* me at the table," Jacob said.

"Matty's *broke*."

"Matty was making ten million dollars a year. What happened to it all? Tandy, listen, he brought this trouble on himself, and now he needs to get his life back. By himself. All of you need to work on getting a life. You can't rely on Peter forever."

What had Jacob just said?

I think time actually stopped. It felt as if a gigantic sinkhole opened between Jacob and me and swallowed up all my belief in him, and my understanding of the world as I knew it.

When time resumed, all I could manage to say was, "What does Peter have to do with this?"

52

I was stunned, thunderstruck, and all my attention was on Jacob. It looked like he wanted to take back what he had said, but it was too late.

I asked him again. "Rely on Peter? What do you mean?"

He said, "For one of the brightest people I've ever met, you can be unbelievably clueless, Tandy."

He walked past me, heading downstairs, and I followed him down the spiral staircase. We passed Mercurio, hooked a right at Robert, and headed for the Pork Chair, which was in the open area behind the lipstick-red sofa and Harry's Pegasus piano.

When Jacob sat down hard in the chair, it grunted and squealed like it was being slaughtered. Any other day, I would have fallen apart, laughing at the surprised look on Jacob's face. But not today.

Uncle Jake recovered his angry face pretty fast and continued his totally unexpected rant.

"Did you ever ask yourself who pays the very pricy monthly charges for this apartment, Tandy? Have you wondered who pays me and Leo, and three private school tuitions, not to mention those thousand-dollar-a-night spa days at Waterside?"

I stared into Jacob's eyes. They were like small twin mirrors reflecting me back to myself, making me say to myself, *How could you be so stupid?*

This breaking news was far worse than I had imagined, but I wanted to make sure I understood. "When we got our inheritance, Phil bought the apartment. Jacob, you said you were rich."

"Right, Tandy. Phil bought the apartment with a one-time multimillion-dollar lump sum from the estate. But there are bills, plenty of them: taxes, common charges, insurance, food, utilities, salaries, and much more.

"Your grandmother didn't know there would be an apartment to buy or tuition or mental health care. She didn't even know that any of you would exist. The money left in her trust for you and your siblings was a 'just in case' plan and, when divided up among you, amounted to about a million dollars each, to be doled out to you in monthly payments until you're fifty-eight years old. That's about two thousand dollars a month.

"It's spend-and-save money. It's hard-times money. But if you get a scholarship to college, if you invest your stipend wisely, it will be a good safety net when you start out in life on your own."

I was hearing this for the first time.

It was a shocking jolt of reality, but it made sense— except for the part about Peter.

My mind raced forward and back and round and round as I examined our relationship with Peter over all the years I had known him. Disdain hardly begins to describe his show of feelings for us.

Jacob was saying, "Peter is carrying you because of his love for your father. He didn't want you to know because he didn't want your thanks. I accepted this guardianship out of loyalty to the family, but I love all of you, Tandy. Even Matthew. I think you know this."

I nodded dumbly as Jacob rested his arms on his knees. I saw the shiny scars on his forearms from the burns he'd suffered while rescuing me from the "accidental" fire, the latest of the three times Jacob had saved my life at risk of his own. No questions about whether he was with *us* or with *Peter* could stand up to those facts.

I got to my feet and he got to his, and I hugged my good uncle, who had sacrificed so much to take care of very difficult kids who totally needed him.

But my mind was blown regarding Uncle Peter.

If I'd been wrong about Peter, then who had been trying to kill us?

NOW OR NEVER

4

53

It was what some might call a lull in the storm.

My tutor, Jackie Rogers, a dean's list student from NYU, wrote to Dr. Oppenheimer saying, "Ms. Angel has gotten perfect test scores, and honestly, she doesn't need me. I recommend she be readmitted to All Saints."

Oppenheimer relented, so I was back at school. Defiantly so.

I wore my old wardrobe with aplomb. I sprayed Tandoori on my underwear, and my expression said *Don't mess with me.* And no one did.

By now, thanks to C.P., my former bestie, everyone knew that I'd spent three of the last four months in a nuthouse. Kids who knew me avoided me. The ones I didn't know stared at me from afar.

I liked that. I wanted to be left alone.

One day during lunch, I left school and walked a couple of blocks along Columbus. I bought a bag of chestnuts from a vendor and was heading back to school when a woman with long brown hair wearing a blue coat grabbed my attention.

She was half a block away, facing away from me, hailing a yellow cab that was coming to a stop.

Was that my sister?

I called out, "Katherine. Katherine, *wait*!"

I had that feeling of déjà vu as I ran toward the woman in the blue coat. But I had no chance to catch her as the cab took off, sending a wave of slush onto the sidewalk.

Had I really seen Kath?

Why would she be in New York and not let me know?

Or was this a sign that my brain had gone off the rails and that I couldn't even trust myself anymore?

I got back to All Saints, still shaken by the possible sighting of my sister, and took a front-row seat in my history class.

When the room was full, Mr. Conroy Brown, my twenty-five-year-old instructor, began his lecture. He was saying that New York, as part of the British imperial trading system, had acquired its mercantile character from Great Britain.

And that was just dead wrong.

As Mr. Brown pontificated, I muttered to myself, still jacked up by seeing a Katherine look-alike on the street.

I was jolted into the moment when Mr. Brown called me out.

"Speak up, Ms. Angel. We all want to hear what you have to say."

That snarky expression must be given out to every graduate in education along with their diplomas, but I was glad of the opportunity to speak up. And I did.

I got to my feet and straightened my shoulders.

"If you were factually accurate," I said, "I would have kept quiet, but since you clearly need my help, I might as well set the record straight."

No one laughed, sneezed, or even exhaled.

Even Mr. Brown seemed paralyzed.

I went on, "So, Mr. Brown, to be fair to the class, the Dutch came to Manhattan well before the British. And they came for one reason—to make a profit. The Dutch named this city New Amsterdam and endowed it with its mercantile character. It's part of our *Dutch* legacy, not British.

"Any questions?"

54

It turns out Mr. Brown did have a question.

His face was a weird, stiff mask of high dudgeon as he asked me, "Do you want to get expelled from school, Ms. Angel?"

"Why would that happen?"

He said, "It would happen because you're rude, insubordinate, and extremely disruptive."

The room had been as quiet as a hole until then, but now there was snickering and raucous laughter. And I'm pretty sure my classmates weren't laughing at me.

"*Not another word*," said the instructor, addressing me and everyone else in the room.

I didn't crack a smile. I locked in on Mr. Brown with my deadly serious gaze—and he blinked first.

"Go to the headmaster's office, *now*," said Mr. Brown, "and wait there. I'll join you when class is over."

I sat down and said, "I'm not going anywhere, Mr. Brown. If the headmaster wants to talk to me, he can come here."

There were claps and even a few whistles, and Mr. Brown slammed a ruler down on his desk and demanded silence. He took his phone and went outside the classroom, where you didn't have to be brilliant to guess that he phoned Oppenheimer and relayed to him what a scourge I was.

When Mr. Brown returned, he gave a shaky lecture on the history of trade in Manhattan. He included the Dutch influence on trade without citing me, and finally, the bell rang.

Students thundered out from behind their desks, and as the classroom emptied, Dr. Oppenheimer waded in.

He was a prim and fussy man with a pinched face who looked to me like his parents had chained him to the radiator as a child until he ate his peas. And that angry little kid had vowed that once he grew up, he would get back at everyone in the world.

I watched his muted back-and-forth conversation with Mr. Brown, and then the two of them advanced upon my front-row desk. Their anger made me feel pretty powerful. I wasn't used to feeling powerful anymore, but I liked it.

"Ms. Angel, you seem bent on destroying your opportunity to attend this school," Oppenheimer said. "You're a smart girl, but not smart enough to make yourself small and avoid scrutiny. Why is that, do you suppose? Looking for drama is my guess. Looking for attention. Which is not a survival trait at All Saints, is it? Think about that, young lady. All Saints is your ticket to your future. This is your very last chance—"

"I don't want a last chance," I cut in, realizing that I'd made a huge snap decision in the last three seconds. "And I don't need your ticket. I'm a person, Dr. Oppenheimer. I have feelings and intelligence, and being small has never been one of my goals.

"In the short time I've known you, Dr. Oppenheimer, you've offended me every time I've seen you. So I'm leaving All Saints, effective this minute. You're *fired*. No second chances for you."

I picked up my bag, and before Oppenheimer could say, "You can't fire *me*," I stalked out of the room and into a small mob of classmates, who put their hands together for Tandy Angel, who was not small at all.

Hugo was there, my irrepressible booster. He hugged me and said, "Way to go, T."

He walked me out to the street, where Harry was leaning against the wrought-iron fence in front of the school, surrounded by fans.

Harry's long hair was thick and shiny, and his shirt was open under his unzipped jacket. His slouchy posture and general lack of starch had taken on a sexy appeal now that he was signing autographs for jumping, squealing girls.

He grinned and waved to me, and I waved back. It was surprising and a little bit hilarious. My twin brother was giving Harry Styles some competition.

I ordered Hugo back to class.

He said, "If *you* don't have to go, *I* don't have to go."

"Hugo. Go to class. You have to get into MIT one day."

I left my brothers at school and walked the few blocks toward home with my mind circling my major preoccupation.

I had an enemy. A dangerous one.

And I had no idea who that enemy was.

55

The San Remo's criminally outdated laundry room is in the vast, cavernous basement, one of many large and small rooms connected by long, dimly lit passageways leading to the stairs and service elevators.

It was late on a weeknight. I was wearing leggings, ballet flats, and one of Matty's winter-weight Giants sweatshirts. I was alone in the laundry room, but the smell of dryer sheets and the hum of the machinery were soothing and homey.

I put a load of whites into a washer and was thinking of dinner as I headed toward the elevators, about forty feet away down a darkened corridor.

I never saw the foot that shot out, tripping and sending

me to the floor, or the hand that grabbed me by the back
of my sweatshirt and pulled me back to my feet.

"*Get off me!*" I screamed, and tried to twist away, but
the crook of a heavy arm clenched around my neck.

A male voice hissed, "Die, bitch."

I saw a flash of metal near my throat, the blade of a knife.
I kicked behind me—a judo self-defense move—and my
foot slammed into a knee. There was a yowl of pain, and I
pushed away and ran like a bomb had gone off behind me.

My slippery shoes flew off my feet as I ran along the
brightest of the dim hallways, past the closed elevator doors. I couldn't stop to push the call button. I just
ran, taking corners when they appeared, afraid that my
attacker would catch up with me any second, screaming
for help as I ran.

I heard footsteps behind me. I think.

There were gigantic industrial fans in the basement ceiling, there to move the heat and static underground air.
Between my screams and the *whack-whack* of the fans,
the echoes of the pumps and furnace, and the rasp of my
own panting, I couldn't be certain I still heard footsteps.
But I did see that blood was dripping from the fingers of
my right hand.

I grabbed my right shoulder as I ran and found a slash
in the sweatshirt a few inches down on the outside of

my right arm. *That bastard cut me.* I kept running, even though I was lost and confused and losing blood.

My bare feet slapped the cement floor as I forced myself onward, yelling "Help!" all the while. I slipped and fell against a stack of empty cartons, then scrambled up and looked around. I didn't see him, and now I realized that I had boxed myself into a dead end—the corner between the bike room and the exit door to the street.

The exit door!

I yanked on the handle and threw my full weight against the door, but it didn't budge. And then I did hear footsteps, echoing against the cement walls and getting closer.

There was nowhere left to go that wouldn't take me directly past my attacker, so I gathered all my fear and rage and braced myself to face him. I would have to fight hard. I would have to kick at his junk, slam an elbow into his throat, use my clasped hands as a club at the back of his neck—and that was when I saw a kitchen knife lying on the ground.

Was it really a knife? *It was.*

I grabbed it up and clutched it. It was long, thin, sharp. It had to be the knife my attacker had used on me, but how had it gotten here? Had he snuck by without me seeing him?

I was trying to catch my breath and get my bearings when I keyed into the footsteps again. The figure of a man materialized from around a bend in the hallway.

I held the knife in front of me with both hands and screamed, "*Get away from me or I'll kill you!*"

The man shouted back, "Who's there?"

And then I recognized Benny, our night doorman.

"Ms. Angel? Was that you screaming?" he asked. "What's wrong? Did someone hurt you?"

Was Benny my attacker? Was he trying to kill me?

He came toward me saying, "Ms. Angel, what happened? Are you hurt?"

Benny was only feet away, his face full of concern. He was sixty and way out of shape. He couldn't have been chasing me.

I held out the knife and said, "Benny, look. Someone used this on me." I pulled at the neckline of my sweatshirt so that he could see the gash below my shoulder.

"You've got blood all over your face."

I touched my chin and cheek, felt where the skin had gotten scraped when I fell—and then I started blubbering. Dammit. I just hate that.

"Benny, thank God you chased him away."

He looked at me strangely. Like, *I did what?*

I said, semihysterically, "Did you see who was after me?"

"I didn't see anybody, Ms. Angel. Maybe you got spooked. Maybe you fell and cut yourself on something?"

"No, Benny. He said, 'Die, bitch.' He cut me with this." Hands shaking, I showed him the knife again, and he shrank away.

"That's sick. Can you walk okay? Here. Lean on me. Let's get you upstairs so your uncle can take you to a doctor."

Benny walked me to the elevator bank, all the while throwing nervous glances at my face and at the knife.

As he repeatedly jabbed the elevator call button, I could tell what he was thinking. He couldn't get this crazy girl off his hands soon enough.

56

It had been a half hour since the murderous thug had slashed me in the basement.

My pulse had slowed to about eighty, but I was still pumping adrenaline. I was panting, sweating, and pressing a washcloth to the slash on the side of my arm, which now hurt like crazy.

Caputo and Hayes sat across the kitchen table from me and Uncle Jacob. The knife between us was spotlighted by the overhead fixture. It was six inches long, with a black handle and a narrow blade that had been sharpened to a razor edge. If I hadn't been wearing Matty's thick sweatshirt, that blade might have sliced my arm to the bone.

Caputo leaned across the table and said, "Let's take it from the top one more time, okay, Brandy?"

"Stop. Doing. That," I said. "I know you're pretending you don't know my name to throw me off. But you're forgetting one thing, Sergeant. I'm not a suspect. I'm the freaking *victim*."

Caputo leaned back, not quite suppressing a smirk. Both he and Hayes were treating me as if I was in the psych ward at Bellevue. Why didn't they write up the incident report and do some detecting? Why didn't they believe me?

Caputo said, "Once again, Tandy. Start at the beginning."

"As I said before, I didn't see him. He came from behind. He tripped me. Then he grabbed at the back of my sweatshirt and pulled me up. He put his arm around my neck. I saw the knife, so I kicked back at his knees. That's when I ran."

"He said something, right?"

"Right. Before I kicked him, he said, 'Die, bitch.' "

"Does that sound familiar to you? Has anyone ever said that before?"

"No."

"Did he call you by name?" Caputo asked.

"No."

"Unlike the guy who took a shot at you on the street?"

That wasn't really a question, so I didn't answer it.

Hayes said, "And this knife? Your, uh, attacker just dropped it?"

"I found it, that's all I know. And I was glad to have it. I thought I would have to use it."

"Too bad you held on to it with your sweaty hands," Caputo mused. "I suppose, if you don't mind waiting about a month, the lab can test it for DNA."

"You should do that," I snapped, "and put a rush on it. I resent your implication that I would cut myself."

Caputo said, "It's a valid hypothesis, Tootsie. Is that what happened? You're desperate to get us to believe you, so you pushed the envelope a little bit—"

I jumped up, losing it, and at the same time not.

"How about getting the security footage from inside the basement and outside the exits? How about interviewing the doormen? Why not see if any other tenants used the laundry room tonight or went down to the garbage room and if they saw anyone they didn't know or who looked suspicious?"

Caputo said to Jacob, "Letting you know. We can't be responding to these kinds of calls anymore."

Jacob said, "Tandy is not a liar."

I shouted at Caputo. "*Someone is trying to kill me!* What are you going to say when you find me dead?"

Chairs scraped. Cops got to their feet. Caputo said,

"If I learn anything, I'll get in touch. Meanwhile, Sandy, maybe you ought to become a writer. Fiction, of course."

"Screw you!" I shouted at Caputo's back.

Jacob gripped my arm to stop me from following the cops to the front door. I felt as crazy as everyone thought I was. Had I fabricated this assault?

My cheek and my chin were scraped from my fall. My arm was cut. I'd heard what I'd heard: "Die, bitch." Footsteps.

Hell, no, I didn't make this up. I don't lie and I'm not crazy. I'm also the leading authority on my own state of mind, thank you.

You can trust me on that.

57

I was still shaky when Jacob and I returned from the emergency room late that night. Hugo was still awake, and he demanded to see the fifteen neat little stitches closing the gash on my arm.

I took a hot shower, then pulled on Harry's pajamas and Hugo's socks for some added comfort. Jacob brought a few of Dr. Robosson's prescribed and newly refilled antianxiety pills up to my bedroom with a cup of herbal tea and a plate of cookies.

I said, "Thanks. And you don't have to watch me swallow the pills. I *want* to take them."

"Good. Do you need anything else right now? I'm going down to the laundry room."

"My whites need to be dried."

"No problem."

"If you see an unknown or imaginary attacker looking for his knife, kindly beat the hell out of him and hold him for questioning."

"Will do. That's a promise."

I swallowed the pills and gathered my two brothers in residence for a meeting on my bed.

I said, "Guys, once again, my sanity is in question. If you think someone threatened and slashed me, please raise your hand."

"We were on the plane together, remember?" Hugo said. "I know a death threat when I see the ground coming up at me."

Harry said, "Seriously? You need a show of hands?"

"Yes. I do."

Hands went up.

"Excellent. Okay. I'm back in detective beast mode. You know my motto: *Mystery solved. Case closed.*"

I repeated to my brothers what Jacob had told me about Peter: that he was supporting our fantastic lifestyle. They were as shocked as I had been, and they had the same questions I had hurled at Jacob.

Why was Peter supporting us when he clearly hated us? And why hadn't we been told?

Harry said, "If he's paying the bills, he could plant spies."

Hugo added, "And spies would tell his hired thugs when to sneak up on you. Like whoever knifed you tonight."

"Agreed," I said. "People we don't even know could be watching. Mailmen. That old couple who are always hanging out in the lobby. By the way, everyone's a suspect until I clear you. Where were you when I was attacked?"

Harry said, "We were both in my room when you went down to do your laundry, goofball. We can alibi each other."

"Okay. You're both not guilty."

I bumped fists first with Harry, then with Hugo.

Hugo said, "*Boooooommmm!*" and shot his fingers out in an "explosion," then rolled off the bed and kept rolling until he hit the wall, where he played dead.

Sometimes I forget he's only eleven. "Get up, Hugo."

"You blew me up," he said. "I saw you."

We all cracked up, and it took a while to call my meeting back to order.

When we'd collected ourselves, I said, "So let's say Peter is guilty of being a pig, but not of trying to kill me. Who else would want me crazy or dead?"

I handed out pads and pens, saying, "Put your number one suspect first, your number two after that, and so on, for a total of five."

After our lists were done, we compared notes and had a heated discussion about the suspects, each of us defending names on the list and providing reasons for other suspects to go to the top.

We firmed up our lists. Then I adjourned the meeting and took a sleeping pill.

Sorry, Dr. Robosson. I have no idea if I dreamed. But when I woke up the next morning, I was breathless, as if I'd been running hard.

Was I fleeing or chasing?

I wish I knew.

CONFESSION

Friend, the names on my list were frightening, even to me. They were people I *knew*, some I've been close to most of my life. And some I hardly knew at all.

Not being able to trust anyone is enough to drive someone crazy. Was that what was happening to me? Had the *pills* finally kicked in with their poison to debilitate me mentally, if not physically? Was I going crazy?

I felt hot tears well up in my eyes. I let them flood and spill over. When I was younger, obediently taking my course of "vitamins" every morning, I never cried. It felt good to have emotions again, even if they were painful and harrowing. But maybe my chaotic thoughts and emotions were hard to manage because I was so out of practice.

My parents had done this to me. And my uncle.

Could I trust anyone ever again?

58

I was in a state of high anxiety the next morning. The pain in my arm reminded me how much I wanted to get ahead of the psycho who had attacked me last night and was still at large.

Hugo, our in-house tech wiz, hacked into the Violent Criminal Apprehension Program and ran a search on our driver, Leonard Peavey. Leo was on Peter's payroll, carried a gun, and knew where I was at all times. He was my number one suspect.

But Leonard Peavey had no criminal history. *Au contraire*. He had been a cop for twenty years in Schenectady, retired with distinction, and became security chief for

Target in Albany before coming to work for us at the age of fifty-five.

He was clean.

We ran a similar search on Philippe Montaigne, our attorney, who had also once worked for Uncle Peter. I ran global searches on Sergeant Capricorn Caputo and Detective Ryan Hayes, and we screened our night doorman, Benito Rodriguez, and the rest of the San Remo staff.

There were no red flags on any of our top suspects, but we continued to throw spaghetti against criminal databases all morning. None of our suspects stuck.

At noon, I decided to call Samantha Peck for help.

Sam, my mother's former personal assistant and—as we'd recently found out—lover, knew the Angel family extremely well, maybe better than I did. She also knew about the plane crash that came *this close* to killing us all and was the reason my brothers and I had missed her mother's funeral.

After we'd exchanged fond hellos, I brought Sam up to the minute on my recent near-death experiences.

"Trust your gut, Sam," I urged her. "Who would want me crazy or dead?"

There was a silence, and then Sam started crying so hard, she couldn't speak. I waited while she blew her nose and went for a glass of water, and when she came back to the phone, she said, "My mother was a mean old bitch, Tandy, but even with her rough edges and hoarding and inappropriate comments and judgments and rudeness, I still miss her. And I miss Maud, too, so much. I even miss Malcolm. I still believe your mom and dad were murdered."

"Sam. You know that's not true."

"I don't know much anymore, sweetie. I'm sorry. I think I've crossed over the line into crazy."

Everything Sam said pulled at my head and my heart in ways I hadn't predicted. I commiserated with our family friend, brought her up to date on my brothers, and finally got her laughing before we said good-bye.

But *I* wasn't laughing.

I sat for a while in my blue room, staring at the sky, remembering my parents' wretched deaths. The end of their lives meant the end of the pills and an epic turning point in the lives of everyone who loved them.

Sirens blaring on Central Park West brought me back to the present. They sounded like a call to action.

I texted Leo and asked him to drive me downtown.

59

I *found Matty sitting on the* steps outside his apartment building, drinking a forty-ounce bottle of Bud. He hadn't shaved in a while. His dreadlocks were so disreputable that they had shot past cool and rolled right up to homeless. He was cheerful, however, and somewhat lucid.

I sat down next to him, facing glinting snowbanks, and I told him everything. He heard me out, including my suspicions.

"Me?" he asked. "Why would I want to kill you?"

"Well, maybe it's not personal. You're prone to violence,

Matty. You have an anger problem, and let's face it, you're a professional thug. And now that you're broke, you could have a financial motive. If the rest of us are out of the way, you might get money from the estate. Or maybe you've got a split personality. I've heard that craziness runs in the family."

Matty laughed and said, "You don't really think I tried to kill you. Come here."

He put his arm around my good shoulder and pulled me close. He hugged me really hard and I liked it. Correction. I *loved* it.

"I never have and never will hurt you, Tandoo. You've been my strongest, most loyal supporter always, and I've loved you since you were born. But I *am* worried about you."

"And I'm kind of worried about *you*, big brother."

I crossed Matty off the list and asked Leo to drive me uptown to Sarabeth's, a trendy tea shop on the Upper East Side.

I was on time. I took a sunny table at a zebra-striped banquette and asked the waiter for lemon cake and peppermint tea. But before I put cup to lip, the door opened with a jangle and James walked in.

He looked like the girl-crush he was, perfectly dressed

to show off his great body and his huge pots of money. He slipped into the seat across from me and said, "Hey, Tandy, you're looking like, uh, someone hit you. Or something."

My heart, traitor that it is, took off at a gallop and sent blood rushing into my cheeks—and down below. But I did my best to seem unaffected by the sight and smell of a boy I still loved.

I said, "I'm okay, James. I'm not going to take up much of your time. I'm not recording this meeting"—his eyebrows shot up at this—"so I want you to be honest with me."

"Not recording? What do you mean?"

"That this conversation is strictly confidential and will never come back to bite you. Oh. Here she is."

The door jangled and C.P. came in. She was in private school slut mode—miniskirt up to her smile, tights, knee-high boots, and an open fur coat over all of that. Skunk, I think. Or hyena.

She sat down next to James and put her hand in his lap, smirking.

I wanted to slap her. But I *had* invited her. Know thy enemy. Keep her close.

Once they'd both ordered tea, I asked, straight-out,

"Does either of you have any idea who may have been responsible for the attempts on my life?"

"Huh?" C.P. said. "What attempts? Oh, I forgot. You're out of your mind."

I ignored her and turned to James.

"James, your father was Uncle Peter's partner for a while. That's a fact. So have you stepped into your father's shoes? Do you have a partnership with my uncle?"

"Me? And your uncle Peter? You can't be serious." Peter was there when I was ripped from James's arms that long-ago night on the beach. At the time, we both had reason to hate him. But that James—the one who cared—was not the boy sitting across from me now.

Screwing the lid tightly closed on those memories, I cut to the chase. "Do you have any idea who might want to kill me?" I asked crisply.

"No, but I think you might be a little grandiose," said James.

"Or delusional," C.P. added. "Megalo-something."

"Megalomaniacal," said James.

C.P. said, "Yeah, that's it." And they both laughed.

I couldn't hide my disgust, so I just went with it.

"Thanks. You've reminded me that neither of you has the brains or the wherewithal to come after me. You're off the list. The tea is on me."

I dropped a fifty on the table and walked out.

"Where to, Ms. Tandy?"

"One Hundred Fifty-Fifth Street and Broadway, please. Thanks, Leo."

I was just about out of suspects.

This would be my last stop.

60

Trinity Church Cemetery is on a sloping twenty-three acres, tucked between banks of nondescript apartment buildings in Washington Heights. It runs downhill between Amsterdam Avenue and Riverside Drive, and from the top of the hill, it owns a commanding view of the Hudson.

I left Leo at the gate and walked uphill under a gray, snow-laden sky to the mausoleum where my parents were interred. It was easy to pick out their final resting place because of the angel statues on each side of the doors and the name Angel carved above the lintel.

I sat on a stone bench fronting the mausoleum, with its view in one direction of the Church of the Intercession and, in the other, of the river. I took in cold breaths and let out frosted ones as snowflakes began to float down.

I was still thinking about my conversation with Sam and felt the ache of irreplaceable loss, maybe more than ever before.

Sam had said, "*My mom was a bitch, but I miss her so much.*"

Maud was worse than a bitch. But now I wasn't thinking of her aloofness or her tough lessons "for my own good." I was remembering lying on the couch with her on Sunday mornings when she did the crossword puzzle in her yellow silk pj's. She asked for my help with the puzzle and shared her tea and toast, and those mornings were so precious, I could almost smell the ink from the *New York Times* and the fragrance of her shampoo.

I was having similar thoughts about my distant and preoccupied father. I saw myself as a little girl, playing in his lab and working with him in the kitchen. He taught me to cook and told me that the best cooks were scientists, whether they knew it or not. Just thinking about him saying that I had a scientific mind made me feel good about myself, then and now.

Sitting there, I decided to relinquish my anger over the stiff punishments and the tight leash and the wretched pills. I even forgave them for my time at Fern Haven,

which was Waterside on steroids, where there were electroshock treatments, heavy medications, and controversial
therapy, all in the interest of getting me away from James.

Looking back, I had to give it to them. They'd been
right about James.

Sweet images came to me of party hats, and ball games
where we watched my big brother take punts and kickoffs
to the house. I thought about growing up with Katherine
and swimming with gentle sharks the size of whales
and about preparing for a future where all of us would
become...something more than just nature and nurture
combined.

I walked up to the gates of the mausoleum and touched
each of the carved stone angels and said, "I know you
loved us in your way and that you did your best. I get that
now, and I'm very grateful. I wish I could talk to you, or
even just see you. I love and miss you both."

And then I let them go.

I found the car on Amsterdam. Leo jumped out and
opened the back door for me. I brushed snow from my
coat and stamped my boots. Then, when I had strapped
in, Leo turned and fixed me with his pale gray eyes.

"Ms. Tandy, I'm asking you again. This isn't bull. Is
there something I can do for you?"

I knew now that Leo used to be a cop. I searched his face for the truth of him and saw nothing to be afraid of.

"Do you mean it?" I said.

"Absolutely," he said. "I'm here for you. Whatever you need. Just ask."

"I need you to tail someone."

"No problem," said Leo. "Who?"

CONFESSION

The nightmare was back again.

The one in which someone—Peter? James? *Malcolm?*—is slowly and firmly pushing my head underwater. I don't know if I'm in a bathtub or a pool or a lake. My guttural screams are abruptly cut off by the water flooding my throat. I fight and flail, but the iron hand steadily, inexorably pushes me down.

I gasp and choke as fluid fills my lungs.

I look up—

61

After a night of tumultuous, haunting dreams, I finally gave up on sleep. I was brushing my teeth, wondering what my parents would advise now that I'd quit school, when Jacob called up to me from downstairs.

"In a minute," I shouted.

"Now," he shouted back.

I was in pajamas—but fine. I went down the stairs, and when I cleared the spiral, I saw a lot of people filling the living room. At eight in the morning?

Harry and Hugo were dressed for school, but their faces were frozen in an expression I could read only as shock. What the hell was going on?

Jacob looked agitated, and that was when I saw that Dr. Robosson, warm and fuzzy in gray cashmere, was sitting in the Pork Chair and two young women were standing behind her.

I knew the women, Luann and Stella, a nurse and an orderly from Waterside. From the corner of my eye, I saw another figure standing between me and the door. I turned my head for a better look.

He was male, white, about twenty-eight, wearing blue scrubs with the name LOUIS stitched over the breast pocket. He had a blond brush cut and fire tattoos spiraling around his huge arms. I had never seen him before.

Dr. Robosson said, "Tandy, don't be afraid. This is a good thing. I want you to come with us to Waterside."

"But why? I'm fine. I'm taking my medicine."

"You had an incident the other night that required stitches. It's been suggested that you may have cut yourself. Honey, just look at what you've done to your face."

I shot a furious look at Jacob and said, "Are you serious? Is this what's happening now? I'm being committed?"

Jacob looked at me helplessly. "I had to call your doctor," he said. "As your guardian, I had to."

Hugo was off the couch like a shot. He had his arms around me and he was saying, "For your own good, Tandy. For your own good."

I unlocked Hugo's arms and started backing away. I knew there was nowhere to go, but I wasn't going down easily. I made a feint toward the kitchen, then an end run around the muscle-bound goon who was still blocking my path to the doorway.

He moved fast—a football player of some type, I could tell. He caught me and twisted my good arm behind my back and lowered me facedown to the floor.

"Honey, please," said Dr. Robosson. She came over to where I was lying and spoke really close to my face. I smelled wintergreen and hair spray. "You *like* Waterside, remember? We're going to take good care of you."

I screamed "*No!*" loud enough to make my shrink pull back and to make my twin brother put his hands over his ears and turn away from me. I lost track of Hugo and Jacob as the orderlies lifted me up and—even as I fought them—strapped me to a gurney.

I yelled, "You can't do this to me! I'm a citizen of the United States!"

I screamed inside the elevator. I shocked the porters, and the doormen and the residents in the lobby. The gurney rattled as it went over the cracks in the sidewalk. Snow swirled around us like ghosts. I called to the people walking past our building, "They're trying to kill me!"

Cell phones came out. Videos were shot.

"I'm being held against my will," I pleaded. "I'm being kidnapped."

A private ambulance with the wavy blue logo of Waterside Center was waiting at the curb. Parked behind the ambulance was our bulletproof car.

Leo got out. He stood beside the open door and tracked me with startled eyes but didn't make a move to help.

"They're doing it, Leo!" I screamed. "Help me, please! They're going to make me *disappear*!"

62

I came out of a deep, thick sleep to find myself in a hospital bed with side rails in a darkened room. I was facing a single casement window. The moon was up, and I recognized the view of the river.

I knew where I was.

This was Waterside, but my room was at an unaccustomed height. I was on a high floor, the psycho ward where the certifiably insane were housed.

It was coming back to me, what had happened that morning. I tried to sit up, but I had so little strength that even using the side bars for leverage didn't help.

I thought at first that I was strapped down, but no.

I'd been drugged.

The heaviness was pinning me to the bed and tamping down whatever emotions that, without the drugs, I would certainly be having. Like justifiable three-alarm fury and overwhelming heartbreak, to name just two.

I was here. Again.

I turned my head to the left and saw amber pill bottles on the nightstand. Some had been tipped over, and pills were scattered everywhere.

What had happened?

Had I fought to stop them from gagging me with pills?

I turned my head to the right, and there, sitting in a chair beside the door, was Leo.

I drew in my breath, a long, sucking gasp.

He put his finger to his mouth, like—*Shhh. Don't scream*. He leaned toward me and said quietly, "It worked, Tandy. You were right."

It was coming back now. All of it.

"I was right? Really?"

Leo nodded, and as muzzy as I was, my head almost exploded. It was as if too much was flooding in—the good and the great; the bad and the horrible. It was cosmic.

"Is it done?" I asked.

"Not yet."

The door to my room opened slowly, and Jacob slipped in as Leo melted into the background. Jacob walked over to my bed and asked softly, "How do you feel, sweetheart?"

"Like I weigh four hundred pounds."

"Can you sit up?"

He put his arm behind me and adjusted the bed.

He said, "I'll help you get dressed. We have to leave now. You've been out of it for the whole day."

Just then, a noise came from the bathroom. Like someone was trying to speak. Leo opened the bathroom door and turned on the light.

"This is Louis," he said to me.

It was the body builder who had been in the apartment this morning, all muscle with flame tattoos wrapping his biceps. Now he was sitting on the floor, subdued, not struggling. I looked at Leo. He showed me a stun gun in his waistband.

Oh.

Jacob brought my clothes from the closet, and I dressed in slow motion while Leo helped Louis to his feet.

"Are we good to go, Lou?"

The man nodded vacantly.

The four of us left the room in pairs.

Groggily, I leaned on Jacob, and we went quietly down six flights of fire stairs. When we reached the ground floor, we ducked through the side door to the garbage room. From there, the outer door opened easily, and we were standing in crisp night air on the tree-lined street lit by the full moon.

As we got into the bulletproof car, I noticed the gray sedan parked behind us. It was a police car.

"Cops?" I asked Jacob.

"Yep. Friends of yours."

I saw Leo transferring Louis to a sergeant I happen to know by heart from ten thousand feet away and in the dark. He was lanky with wild dark hair, his pant cuffs hanging above his ankles and his zodiac goat tattooed on his wrist.

Sergeant Caputo gave me a little wave.

Bemused, I waved back.

Doors slammed. Headlights flashed on. Leo got behind the wheel of the bulletproof car, and both vehicles moved away from the curb.

Jacob said, "Tandy, this could get rough. Emotionally and physically. Are you sure you're ready for this?"

I nodded.

As we drove down the halogen-lit West Side Highway, my uncle Jacob told me all that he knew.

My nerve endings were tingling. My brain was humming with good vibrations. This was going to be an evening to remember always.

I was about to solve my greatest mystery.

63

I was still woozy and nauseous from the load of drugs in my system when our car pulled up to the curb on Eighty-First near Columbus and parked in front of an apartment building that I recognized all too well.

Caputo and Hayes parked their unmarked gray Chevy sedan behind us. Caputo transferred Louis, the handcuffed orderly, to another unmarked car across the street while Hayes opened my door and helped me out to the sidewalk. I hung on to his arm to steady myself.

He said, "Tandy, we'll be with you the whole time, okay? Mr. Peavey, if you don't mind, stay here and keep your phone line open."

Jacob, Caputo, Hayes, and I entered the foyer of the

posh apartment building, where Caputo badged the doorman and said, "Police. Call up to Mr. Angel and tell him that his brother, Jacob, is here to see him. Nothing else."

I flashed on the last time I'd seen my loathsome uncle as the elevator ascended and we four approached the door at the end of the hall.

Caputo indicated to Jacob to come right to the door, while the rest of us flattened ourselves against the wall.

Is this really happening?

Are the police really at Peter's door?

Jacob rang the doorbell. Locks clacked, and the door opened wide enough to accommodate Peter's face. He was wild-haired and wild-eyed as he looked at Jacob and snapped, "What's this about, Jake? I have company. It's midnight, for Christ's sake."

Caputo stepped forward, showed Peter his badge, and said, "I'm Sergeant Caputo. This is my partner, Detective Hayes. Mind inviting us in for a minute or two?"

That was when Peter saw me. His eyes widened, but then he scoffed, flung open the door, and said, "Jacob, you're a damned fool. What wild story has my niece been telling you now? I suppose she's been accusing me of trying to murder her. And now the police are involved? Bad move, brother."

I held back snarky retorts in the interest of letting the

police run this show. We followed Peter into the apartment, through the foyer, and into the barely furnished living room.

Hayes said, "Mind if I take a look around?" He went directly to the closed doors beyond Peter's desk.

"Of course I mind. You didn't answer my question," said Peter. "What's this about?"

Caputo pulled a folded paper from his inside pocket. "This is an arrest warrant, Mr. Angel. As a matter of fact, I have two of them."

Hayes knocked on the bedroom door. A woman's voice said, "Peter?"

"It's the police, ma'am. Please step outside."

Peter's face was flushed as he said, "What is this trumped-up whatever? I'm under arrest for *what*, exactly?"

"As you said," Caputo said, "you're under arrest for the attempted murder of your niece. Put your hands behind your back, Mr. Angel."

The bedroom door opened, and I clawed my hands down my face. I was glad to be right, but at the same time, this was the worst betrayal, *ever*. I'd asked Leo to follow the one person who knew my movements to the minute, who understood the workings of my mind, maybe better than I knew them myself.

"Peter, what's going on?" asked Dr. Mary Robosson.

She was wearing a Waterside Center robe and her hair was bunched in a messy ponytail, making her look completely alien to me. She seemed strangely composed.

Hayes said, "You're under arrest as well, Dr. Robosson."

"Do *not* touch me," she said.

I wanted to feel something—rage, jubilance, ecstasy—but I was still numb and nauseated from the damned drugs.

This was emotional robbery.

Peter's fury, however, was obvious. He said to me, "You wretched girl. I'll sleep in my own bed tonight, but I'm officially done with you and your idiot brothers, Tandoori. My checkbook is closed. You have nothing on me but your hysterical, girlish imagination—no evidence, no proof, no *nothing*."

I cleared my throat a couple of times.

Then I said, "Actually, we have something—your girlfriend and coconspirator. We also have her hired thug. If she's offered a deal, I think she's going take it, Uncle Peter. She has no conscience. I think she'll tell us everything."

64

We *were at the Twentieth Precinct,* sitting around the scarred metal table in the break room.

Peter and Dr. Robosson had been charged with conspiracy to commit murder. While they were chilling out in separate interrogation rooms, Leo, Jacob, and I sipped cold coffee with Caputo and Hayes and tried to fit the pieces together. It was a high: three cops, a former Mossad intelligence officer, and me, a seventeen-year-old former high school student who had, as Caputo said, "earned a seat at the table."

I was thinking, *Thanks, Cappy. That's not quite an apology*—but I didn't say it. He had finally collared my monstrous uncle, as well as my wretched shrink.

As an added bonus, Robosson's killer for hire, Louis Caltrane, was in a cell because Leo had caught him "holding the bag"—an IV bag of sedatives, that is. An overdose that was meant to kill me.

Leo was running the story again, how after my cemetery visit, he'd followed Dr. Robosson to a coffee shop, where she had met Uncle Peter. Leo had taken a booth behind them and listened as they discussed "a permanent solution to the Tandy problem."

Their plan was too easy.

They decided that after my next therapy session, she would check me into Waterside for observation. And then my dear uncle Peter, my father's brother, my own blood relative, had suggested to his lover, "I think Tandy will commit suicide, don't you?"

The coffee was coming on and the drugs were wearing off. I knew this because listening to how Dr. Robosson and my uncle had plotted to murder me sent a jolt of pure white fury right through me. I could have flipped the table. I could have flipped a *car*.

But I forced myself to be quiet while Jacob explained that the so-called intervention in our living room had been my idea. It had given Dr. Robosson and Uncle Peter the chance they were looking for to lock me up at Waterside, while giving us an opportunity to take control of their plan.

Leo continued his story by saying that he had followed the ambulance to Waterside, where Caputo and Hayes talked to the management, who gave Leo scrubs, a name tag, and cover. He'd gone to the seventh floor, where he'd introduced himself to Louis as a new hire, and then he'd watched my room.

Leo said to me, "Robosson gave you a sedative right away, but your vital signs were all good. So while you slept, I helped Louis mop floors, and when he prepared your overdose, I busied myself cleaning the bathroom. Christ, I had to wait until he had emptied all the drug bottles on the bedside table and had the IV needle in his hand."

He shook his head, remembering.

"That's when I took him down," Leo said. "I roughed him up a little until he spilled."

"A pretty good move," said Caputo. "Hats off, buddy."

"Outstanding," I said. "Then what happened?"

Leo said, "Louis told me that Dr. Robosson paid him 'a bomb' to kill you, Tandy, and to make it look like a suicide. He said that Dr. R. was working with her 'boy-friend'; he didn't know the guy's name."

Leo went on. "I secured Louis in the bathroom. Then I gloved up, bagged the IV bag in a clean trash bag, and left the empty bottles on the table, so as to preserve the evidence."

Caputo picked up where Leo left off. He said, "Louis's statement will indict Dr. Robosson, but all we have on Peter is an overheard conversation. It's hearsay. If we want to hold Peter, the doctor is going to have to implicate him by name and on the record."

Hayes said, "Cappy's going to interrogate Peter. And while he's doing that, Tandy, if you're willing, you could have a private chat with Dr. Robosson. I'll be right behind the glass."

65

The interrogation room *was the size* of a walk-in closet, furnished with a metal table, four chairs, a two-way mirror, a light fixture, and a camera in a corner of the ceiling.

Dr. Robosson was sitting at the table, wearing the clothes she'd worn yesterday: a tan gabardine suit, a silk blouse with a stain on it, and diamond studs.

She looked up when I opened the door.

"Oh, Tandy. I thought you were those horrible cops. Where are they?"

"Interrogating Peter and Louis, I think. I shouldn't be here, but we have to talk. Don't you agree, you heinous bitch?"

I pulled out a chair and sat down.

"Of course. Tell me what you're feeling," she said. Like this was a therapy session and she was still my doctor.

"I feel glad to be alive," I said. "But how do *you* feel about yourself, Doctor? I trusted you more than anyone in the world, and you betrayed that trust completely."

"It's not what you think," she said.

"No? You aren't sleeping with my uncle? You didn't conspire with him to kill me?"

"Tandy, yes, I've been seeing Peter since you first came to Waterside. You were convinced that he was out to kill you, and I had to see for myself."

"And one thing led to another?" I said.

"It's a cliché, but that's right. We did connect over concern for you. We fell in love."

I guess I thought she'd be furious, or apologetic or ashamed—*something*. But her affect was flat. Like this was happening to someone else.

"Is that ethical?" I asked. "Are you allowed to sleep with a patient's close family member without telling them?"

"Strictly speaking, there's nothing unethical about it. Peter is not your parent or boyfriend or child. But I can see how you might find it uncomfortable."

Uncomfortable? She was delusional—or worse. How had I missed this?

"You've got your uncle all wrong, you know," she said. "He's a good man, Tandy. A big thinker. A humanitarian."

"Peter is a humanitarian? Is that right?"

"You think the pills damaged you, when everyone knows that you and your siblings are extraordinary. Don't you see that if those pills were readily available, they would benefit other children, and that that would be a tremendous asset to all of mankind? You were trying to stop that."

"The pills kill your emotions," I said. "Is it a benefit for mankind to have no feelings, no conscience? You're a psychiatrist, for God's sake."

"I've had a real breakthrough since I met Peter. I see now that emotions impede success in life. They cause broken homes and destroy marriages and damage children. I should know. I've been a practicing therapist for twenty years. Has talk therapy helped you, Tandy?"

I couldn't answer her. Surely talk therapy with her had been a total sham.

"I started taking the pills, Tandy. Yes, *me*—and they've given me wonderful clarity."

"I'm not following you," I said, dropping a hunk of bait into the trap.

"It's simple, Tandy. Look. If you'd gotten your way, Angel Pharmaceuticals might have closed. The ground-breaking work your father and Peter have done would be lost along with the promise of pure analytical thinking for millions who need clear minds to survive in this challenged world."

Dr. Robosson was glowing. She was high on a mission that overrode common sense. Talk about drinking the Kool-Aid...did this clueless freaking maniac know what she was saying?

"I tried to help you, Tandy, but you wouldn't leave it alone. So you had to be sacrificed. One person for the greater good of humanity. You see that now, don't you?"

Not really. She was mentally disintegrating in front of my eyes. Had the shame of getting caught caused Dr. Robosson to have a psychotic break? Had the pills done this to her? Had Peter brainwashed her? Or had she been freaking crazy all along?

"Okay, let me see if I've got this right. You're saying that when Peter's attempts to kill me failed, you decided to get me out of the way. For the common good."

She smiled agreeably. "You would have just drifted off to sleep."

That was an admission of wrongdoing.

The trap slammed shut.

It took everything I had not to look up at the camera. I got out of my chair and stood over her.

"I've had a breakthrough, Dr. Robosson. I just realized you're a psychopath. Like my uncle Peter. Thanks for the session."

I stalked out of the interrogation room and ran right into Hayes. He grabbed my shoulders, then shook my hand.

"You did it," he said. "Nailed her like a pro."

"What about Peter?"

"He's asked for his lawyer."

Crap. No doubt Peter would hire the best lawyer in New York, who could get him off.

5

THE BEST DAY OF MY LIFE

66

Months had passed since the conspiracy to kill me at Waterside Center had been thwarted. Now it was a warm summer evening in Manhattan, a long holiday weekend in July.

Leo was at the wheel, Uncle Jake was riding shotgun, and the rest of us were in the backseats of the long black car: me and Harry, Hugo, Matthew, and Kath, along with her baby son, George.

Yes, *Katherine*. My brave, sweet, wonderful big sister, who no longer had to hide her very existence from our uncle Peter.

It's been said that the wheels of justice grind slowly, but Matthew's lawsuit against the owner of our crashed aircraft had been quickly settled in our favor, and we were paying our own bills now.

Dr. Robosson agreed to testify against Peter in exchange for a lighter sentence and was now residing at Bedford Hills Correctional Facility, working off her next ten years, one slow day at a time.

Peter's trial date was still in the indeterminate future, but until then, he was being held without bail at Rikers Island. Most importantly, he no longer owned Angel Pharmaceuticals.

Philippe Montaigne, our family lawyer, good friend, and protector, produced the founding documents that my parents and Peter had prepared and signed twenty-five years ago. Despite the change of management due to the company's short-lived bankruptcy, once Peter resumed ownership, the original regulations were reinstated. Namely, that in the event none of the founders were available to run the company, control would pass to a committee of their offspring. By unanimous decision, my siblings elected me CEO of Angel Pharmaceuticals with fifty-one percent of the voting shares.

I had voted—and my siblings had gone along with me.

That was why we were all together now, heading downtown toward a gray concrete-slab factory in Hell's Kitchen as dusk settled over the city.

Our excitement was palpable as Leo slowed the car and pulled into an empty parking lot two blocks east of the Angel Pharmaceuticals plant. From this spot, we had a clear view of the factory, which was dark and empty on a Sunday evening.

Jacob and Leo opened the car doors and we all got out, breathless with anticipation. Speaking for myself, I was also a little bit fearful.

Harry put it into words.

"This might be the craziest thing you've done yet, Tandy. There are so many options that make more sense."

"I know," I said. "But this puts an end to this dirty business forever. I'm not going to regret it."

"No regrets here, either, Tandoo," said Katherine. "Nothing but blood money came from that horrible place."

She put her arm around my waist, and we lined up in a row facing Angel Pharmaceuticals.

Jacob looked at his watch.

"Ten seconds and counting," he said.

I grinned at him and he grinned back. We bumped fists, and of course, Hugo said, "*Boooommmm!*"

It was as if Hugo had pressed the detonator himself. Small controlled explosions erupted on several floors of the building like the beginning of a fireworks display.

All of us said "*Boom,*" even Leo and Uncle Jake.

And then, with sharp crackling sounds and huge clouds of dust, the whole freaking building crumpled, folding in on itself, and Angel Pharma, along with too many family nightmares to count, once and for all came tumbling down.

In the eerie aftermath of the explosions, as the dust clouds blended with the darkening sky, there was a surprising moment of silence. As Dr. Robosson had said, my father's dreams and Peter's had materialized in this place, and now all that was left of their terrible experiments were our wounded hearts and terrible memories.

I saw that Harry had tears on his cheeks. I hoped this was the end of his deeply felt grief at being the least-loved child.

And then the breeze coming off the Hudson River blew off the momentary sadness. I was filled with exhilaration. I felt liberated, as though Independence Day was inside *me*.

I was actually free.

My siblings and I whooped and embraced one another, and Matty cracked open a bottle of champagne and poured it over my head. More corks popped, and we all laughed and danced like fools in the delicious sparkling rain. I loved everyone here.

The wide-open views of the West Side of New York were wider and more open now that Angel Pharmaceuticals was rubble.

My God.

This was truly the best day of my life—so far. And I'm not done yet, not even *close*. But I know this right now. No other kids will take Angel Pharmaceuticals' heinous, unpredictable, brain-changing "vitamin pills" ever again.

And that's all I ever really wanted.

Game *over*. Case closed.

Wishing you the best of everything.

Your friend,

Tandoori Angel

ACKNOWLEDGMENTS

Our thanks to John A. Duffy for his touching lyrics, pilot Pete Colomello for his super aerodynamics, attorney Philip R. Hoffman for weighing in on the law, and Ingrid Taylar for her thorough research.

AXI MOORE IS A GOOD GIRL.
BUT NOW, SHE'S RUNNING AWAY
FROM HER OLD LIFE AND LEAVING ON
THE ROAD TRIP OF A LIFETIME.

And she's ready to fall in love.

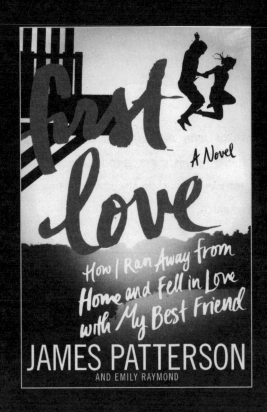

first love

A Novel

How I Ran Away from
Home and Fell in Love
with My Best Friend

JAMES PATTERSON
and EMILY RAYMOND

READ ON FOR AN EXTRACT

1

IT WAS 4:30 A.M. WHEN I WOKE UP AND
pulled my backpack out from under the bed. I'd spent the last
few nights obsessively packing and unpacking and repacking it,
making sure I had exactly what I needed and no more: a couple
of changes of clothes, Dr. Bronner's castile soap (good for
"Shave-Shampoo-Massage-Dental-Soap-Bath," says the label),
and a Swiss Army knife that I'd swiped from my dad's desk
drawer. A camera. And, of course, my journal, which I carry
everywhere.

Oh, and more than fifteen hundred dollars in cash, because
I'd been the neighborhood's best babysitter for going on five
years now, and I charged accordingly.

Maybe there was a part of me that always knew I was going
to split. I mean, why else didn't I blow my money on an iPad
and a Vera Wang prom dress, like all the other girls in my

class? I'd had that map of the US on my wall for ages, and I'd stare at it and wonder what Colorado or Utah or Michigan or Tennessee is like.

I can't believe it took me as long as it did to get up the guts to leave. After all, I'd watched my mom do it. Six months after my little sister, Carole Ann, died, Mom wiped her red-rimmed eyes and took off. Went back East where she'd grown up, and as far as I know, never looked back.

Maybe the compulsion to run away is genetic. Mom did it to escape her grief. My dad escapes with alcohol. Now I was doing it…and it felt strangely *right*. At long last. I could almost forgive Mom for splitting.

I slipped on my traveling clothes and sneakers—saying good-bye to my favorite boots—and hoisted my backpack onto my shoulder, cinching the straps tight. I was going to miss this apartment, this town, this *life*, like an ex-con misses his jail cell, which is to say: Not. At. All.

My dad was asleep on the ugly living room couch. It used to have these pretty pink flowers on it, but now they look sort of brownish orange, like even fabric plants could die of neglect in our apartment. I walked right by and slipped out the front door.

My dad gave a small snort in his sleep, but other than that, he never even stirred. In the last few years, he'd gotten pretty used to people leaving. Would it really matter if another member of the Moore family disappeared on him?

Out in the hallway, though, I paused. I thought about him waking up and shuffling into the kitchen to make coffee. He'd see how clean I'd left it, and he'd be really grateful, and maybe he'd decide to come home from work early and actually cook us a family dinner (or a what's-left-of-the-family dinner). And then he'd wait for me at the table, the way I'd waited so many nights for him, until the food got cold.

Eventually, it would dawn on him: I was gone.

A dull ache spread in my chest. I turned and went back inside.

Dad was on his back, his mouth slightly open as he breathed, his shoes still on. I put out a hand and touched him lightly on the shoulder.

He wasn't a horrible father, after all. He paid the rent and the grocery bill, even if it was me who usually did the shopping. When we talked, which wasn't often, he asked me about school and friends. I always said everything was great, because I loved him enough to lie. He was doing the best he could, even if that best wasn't very good.

I'd written about eight hundred drafts of a good-bye note. The Pleading One: *Please try to understand, Dad, this is just something I have to do.* The Flattering One: *It's your love and concern for me, Dad, that give me the strength to make this journey.* The Literary One: *As the great Irish playwright George Bernard Shaw wrote, "Life isn't about finding yourself. Life is about creating yourself." And I want to go create myself, Dad.* The Pissy One: *Don't worry about me, I'm good at taking care of myself. After all, I've been doing it since Mom left.* In the end, though, none of them seemed right, and I'd thrown them all away.

I bent down closer. I could smell beer and sweat and Old Spice aftershave.

"Oh, Daddy," I whispered.

Maybe there was a tiny part of me that hoped he'd wake up and stop me. A small, weak part that just wanted to be a little girl again, with a family that wasn't sick and broken. But *that* sure wasn't going to happen, was it?

So I leaned in and kissed my father on the cheek. And then I left him for real.

2

ROBINSON WAS WAITING FOR ME IN THE back booth of the all-night diner on Klamath Avenue, two blocks from the bus station. Next to him was a backpack that looked like he'd bought it off a train-hopping hobo for a chicken and a nickel, and his face made me think of a watchdog resting with one eye open. He looked up at me through the steam rising from his coffee.

"I ordered pie," he said.

As if on cue, the waitress delivered a gooey plate of blueberry pie and two forks. "You two are up early," she said. It was still dark. Not even the birds were awake yet.

"We're vampires, actually," Robinson said. "We're just having a snack before bed." He squinted at her name tag and then smiled his big, gorgeous smile at her. "Don't tell on us, okay, Tiffany? I don't need a stake through my heart. I'm only five hundred years old—*way* too young and charming to die."

She laughed and turned to me. "Your boyfriend's a flirt," she said.

"Oh, he's not my boyfriend," I said quickly.

Robinson's response was almost as quick. "She asked me out, but I turned her down."

I kicked him under the table and he yelped. "He's lying," I told her. "It's the other way around."

"You two are a comedy act," Tiffany said. She wasn't that much older than we were, but she shook her head like we were silly kids. "You should take that show on the road."

Robinson took a big bite of pie. "Believe me, we're gonna," he said.

He shoved the plate toward me, but I shook my head. I couldn't eat. I'd managed to keep a lid on my nerves, but now I felt like jumping out of my skin. When had I ever done anything this crazy, this monumental? I never even broke my curfew.

"Hurry up with that pie," I said. "The bus to Eureka leaves in forty-five minutes."

Robinson stopped chewing and stared at me. "Pardon?"

"The *buuuuus*," I said, drawing it out. "You know, the one we're getting on? So we can get the heck out of here?"

Robinson cracked up, and I considered kicking him again, because it doesn't take a genius to tell the difference between being laughed *with* and laughed *at*. "What's so funny?"

He leaned forward and put his hands on mine. "Axi, Axi, Axi," he said, shaking his head. "This is the trip of a lifetime. We are *not* going to take it on a Greyhound bus."

"What? Who's in charge of this trip, anyway?" I demanded. "And what's so bad about a bus?"

Robinson sighed. "*Everything* is bad about a bus. But I'll give you some specifics so you'll stop looking at me with those big blue eyes. This is *our* trip, Axi, and I don't want to share it with a dude who just got out of prison or an old lady who wants to show me pictures of her grandkids." He pointed a forkful of pie at me. "Plus, the bus is basically a giant petri dish for growing superbacteria, and it takes way too long to get anywhere. Those are your two bonus reasons."

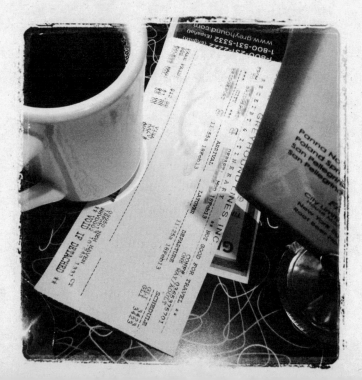

I threw up my hands. "Last I checked, we don't have a private jet, Robinson."

"Who said anything about a plane? We're going to take a car, you dope," he said. He leaned back in the booth and crossed his hands behind his head, totally smooth and nonchalant. "And I do mean *take* one."

3

"WHAT ARE YOU *DOING*?" I HISSED AS ROB-
inson led us down one of the nearby side streets. His legs are
about twice as long as mine, so I had to jog to keep up with
him.

When we came to an intersection, I grabbed his arm and
whirled him around to face me. Eye to eye. Scalawag to Ms.
Straitlaced.

"Are you serious about this?" I said. "Tell me you're not
serious."

He smiled. "You took care of the route. Let me take care of
the ride."

"Robinson—"

He shook off my grip and slung his arm around my shoulder, big brother–style. "Now settle down, GG, and I'll give you
a little lesson in vehicle selection."

"A lesson in *what*? And don't call me that." It stands for Good Girl, and it drives me absolutely nuts when he says it.

Robinson pointed to a car just ahead. "Now that, see, is a Jaguar. It's a beautiful machine. But it's an XJ6, and those things have problems with their fuel filters. You can't have your stolen car leaking gas, Axi, because it could catch on fire, and if you don't die a fiery death, well, you're definitely going to jail for grand theft auto."

We walked on a little farther, and he pointed to a green minivan. "The Dodge Grand Caravan is roomy and dependable, but we're adventurers, not soccer moms."

I decided to pretend this was all make-believe. "Okay, what about that one?" I asked.

He followed my finger and looked thoughtful. "Toyota Matrix. Yeah, definitely a good option. But I'm looking for something with a bit more flair."

By now the sun was peeking over the horizon, and the birds were up and chattering to each other. As Robinson and I walked down the leafy streets, I felt the neighborhood stirring. What if some guy stepped outside to grab the newspaper and saw us, two truants, suspiciously inspecting the neighborhood cars?

"Come on, Robinson," I said. "Let's get out of here." I was still hoping we'd make the bus. We had ten minutes left.

"I just want the perfect thing," he said.

At that moment, we saw a flash in the corner of our eyes. It was white and fast and coming toward us. I gasped and reached out for Robinson.

He laughed and pulled me close. "Whoa, Axi, get a grip. It's only a dog."

My heart was thrumming. "Yeah, I can see that...now."

I could also now see it wasn't likely to be an attack dog, either. He was a small thing, with short, patchy fur. No collar, no tags. I took a step forward, my hand extended, and the dog flinched. He turned around and went right up to Robinson instead (of course) and licked his hand. Then the darn thing lay down at his feet. Robinson knelt to pet him.

"Robinson," I said, getting impatient, "Greyhound bus or stolen car, the time is now."

He didn't seem to hear me. His long, graceful hands gently tugged on the dog's ears, and the dog rolled onto his side. As Robinson scratched the dog's belly, the animal's leg twitched and his pink tongue lolled out of his little mouth in total canine ecstasy.

"You're such a good boy," Robinson said gently. "Where do you belong?"

Even though the dog couldn't answer, we knew. He was skinny and his fur was clumped with mud. There was a patch of raw bare skin on his back. This dog was no one's dog.

"I wish you could come with us," Robinson said. "But we have a long way to go, and I don't think you'd dig it."

The dog looked at him like he'd dig anything in the world

as long as it involved more petting by Robinson. But when you're running away from your life and you can't take anything you don't need, a stray dog falls in the category of Not Necessary.

"Give him a little love, Axi," Robinson urged.

I bent down and dug my fingers into the dog's dirty coat the way I'd seen Robinson do, and when I ran my hand down the dog's chest, I could feel the quick flutter of his heart, the excitement of finding a home, someone to care for him.

Poor thing, I thought. Somehow, I knew exactly what he was feeling. He had no one, and he was stuck here.

But we weren't. Not anymore.

"We're leaving, little buddy. I'm sorry," I said. "We've just got to go."

It was totally weird, but for some reason that good-bye hurt almost as much as the one I'd whispered to my father.

4

WE LEFT THE DOG WITH ONE OF Robinson's sticks of beef jerky, then headed to the end of the block, where Robinson pulled up short. "There it is," he whispered, with real awe in his voice. He grabbed my hand and we hurried through the intersection.

"There *what* is?" I asked, but of course he didn't answer me.

If things went on like this, we'd have to have a little talk—because I didn't want a traveling companion who paid attention to 50 percent of whatever came out of my mouth. If I wanted to be ignored, I could just stay in Klamath Falls with my idiotic classmates and my alcoholic father.

"There is the answer," Robinson said finally, sighing so big you'd have thought he just fell in love. He turned to me and bent down in an exaggerated bow, sweeping his arm out like a valet at some superfancy restaurant (the kind of place we don't have in K-Falls).

"Alexandra, milady, your chariot awaits," Robinson said with a wild grin. I rolled my eyes at him, like I always do when he does this fake-British shtick with my full name.

And then I rolled my eyes again: my so-called chariot, it turned out, was actually a *motorcycle*. A big black Harley-Davidson with yards of shining chrome, and two black leather side bags decorated with silver grommets. There were tassels on the handlebars and two cushioned seats. The thing gleamed like it was straight off the showroom floor.

Robinson was beside me, whispering in some foreign language. "Twin Cam Ninety-Six V-Twin," he said, then something about "electronic throttle control and six-speed transmission" and then a bunch of other things I didn't understand.

It was an amazing bike, even I could see that, and I can hardly tell a dirt bike from a Ducati. "Awesome," I said, checking my watch. "But we *really* should keep moving."

That was when I realized Robinson was bending toward the thing with a screwdriver in his hand.

"Are you out of your *mind*?" I hissed.

But Robinson didn't answer me. Again.

He was going to *hot-wire* the thing. *Holy s—*

I ran to the other side of the street and ducked down between two cars. Adrenaline rushed through my veins and I pressed my eyes shut.

There was no way this was happening, I told myself. No way he was going to actually get the thing started, no way this was how our journey would begin.

I had it all planned out, and it looked nothing like this.

Then the roar of an engine split open the quiet morning. I opened my eyes and a second later Robinson's feet appeared, one on either side of the Harley.

We're breaking the law! I should have screamed. But my mind simply couldn't process this change in plans. I couldn't say anything at all. I just thought: *He's running away in cowboy boots! That is so not practical!* And: *Why didn't I bring mine?*

"Stand up, Axi," Robinson yelled. "Get on."

I was rooted to the spot, my chest tight with anxiety. I was going to have a heart attack right here on Cedar Street, in between a pickup and a Volvo with a MY OTHER CAR IS A BROOM bumper sticker. So much for my great escape!

But then Robinson reached down and hauled me up, and the next thing I knew I was sitting behind him on the throbbing machine with the engine revving.

"Put your arms around me," he yelled.

I was so heart-and-soul terrified that I did.

"Now hang on!"

He put the thing in gear and we took off, the engine thundering in my ears. My dad was probably going to wake up on the couch and wonder if he'd just heard the rumble of an early-summer storm.

We shot past the Safeway, past the high school football field, past the Reel M Inn Tavern, where every Friday night my dad hooked himself up to a Budweiser IV, and past the "Mexican" restaurant (where they put Parmesan cheese on top of their burritos).

Yeah, Klamath Falls. It was the kind of place that looked best in a rearview mirror.

Seeing it flash past me, feeling the rush of the wind in my face, I suddenly didn't care if we woke up the entire stinking town.

Eat my dust! I wanted to shout.

Robinson let out a joyful whoop.

We'd done it. We were free.

CONTINUE THE JOURNEY IN

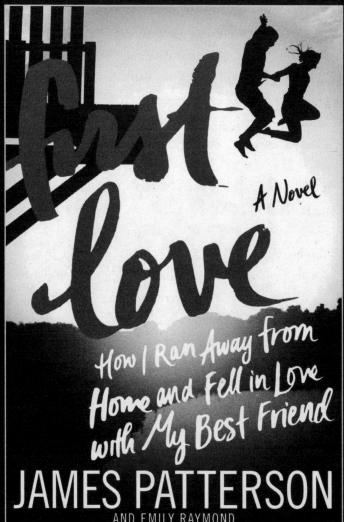

first love

A Novel

How I Ran Away from Home and Fell in Love with My Best Friend

JAMES PATTERSON

AND EMILY RAYMOND

Also by James Patterson

ALEX CROSS NOVELS

Along Came a Spider • Kiss the Girls • Jack and Jill •
Cat and Mouse • Pop Goes the Weasel • Roses are Red •
Violets are Blue • Four Blind Mice • The Big Bad Wolf •
London Bridges • Mary, Mary • Cross • Double Cross •
Cross Country • Alex Cross's Trial (*with Richard DiLallo*) •
I, Alex Cross • Cross Fire • Kill Alex Cross • Merry Christmas,
Alex Cross • Alex Cross, Run • Cross My Heart • Hope to Die •
Cross Justice • Cross the Line

THE WOMEN'S MURDER CLUB SERIES

1st to Die • 2nd Chance (*with Andrew Gross*) •
3rd Degree (*with Andrew Gross*) • 4th of July (*with Maxine Paetro*) •
The 5th Horseman (*with Maxine Paetro*) • The 6th Target (*with
Maxine Paetro*) • 7th Heaven (*with Maxine Paetro*) •
8th Confession (*with Maxine Paetro*) • 9th Judgement (*with
Maxine Paetro*) • 10th Anniversary (*with Maxine Paetro*) •
11th Hour (*with Maxine Paetro*) • 12th of Never (*with
Maxine Paetro*) • Unlucky 13 (*with Maxine Paetro*) •
14th Deadly Sin (*with Maxine Paetro*) • 15th Affair (*with
Maxine Paetro*)

DETECTIVE MICHAEL BENNETT SERIES

Step on a Crack (*with Michael Ledwidge*) •
Run for Your Life (*with Michael Ledwidge*) •
Worst Case (*with Michael Ledwidge*) •
Tick Tock (*with Michael Ledwidge*) •
I, Michael Bennett (*with Michael Ledwidge*) •
Gone (*with Michael Ledwidge*) •
Burn (*with Michael Ledwidge*) •
Alert (*with Michael Ledwidge*) •
Bullseye (*with Michael Ledwidge*)

PRIVATE NOVELS

Private (*with Maxine Paetro*) • Private London (*with Mark Pearson*) •
Private Games (*with Mark Sullivan*) • Private: No. 1 Suspect (*with
Maxine Paetro*) • Private Berlin (*with Mark Sullivan*) • Private Down
Under (*with Michael White*) • Private L.A. (*with Mark Sullivan*) •
Private India (*with Ashwin Sanghi*) • Private Vegas (*with Maxine Paetro*)
• Private Sydney (*with Kathryn Fox*) • Private Paris (*with Mark Sullivan*)
• The Games (*with Mark Sullivan*)

NYPD RED SERIES

NYPD Red (*with Marshall Karp*) •
NYPD Red 2 (*with Marshall Karp*) •
NYPD Red 3 (*with Marshall Karp*) •
NYPD Red 4 (*with Marshall Karp*)

STAND-ALONE THRILLERS

Sail (*with Howard Roughan*) • Swimsuit (*with Maxine Paetro*) • Don't
Blink (*with Howard Roughan*) • Postcard Killers (*with Liza Marklund*) •
Toys (*with Neil McMahon*) • Now You See Her (*with Michael Ledwidge*) •
Kill Me If You Can (*with Marshall Karp*) • Guilty Wives (*with
David Ellis*) • Zoo (*with Michael Ledwidge*) • Second Honeymoon (*with
Howard Roughan*) • Mistress (*with David Ellis*) • Invisible (*with David
Ellis*) • The Thomas Berryman Number • Truth or Die (*with Howard
Roughan*) • Murder House (*with David Ellis*) • Never Never (*with
Candice Fox*) • Woman of God (*with Maxine Paetro*)

NON-FICTION

Torn Apart (*with Hal and Cory Friedman*) •
The Murder of King Tut (*with Martin Dugard*)

ROMANCE

Sundays at Tiffany's (*with Gabrielle Charbonnet*) •
The Christmas Wedding (*with Richard DiLallo*) •
First Love (*with Emily Raymond*)

OTHER TITLES

Miracle at Augusta (*with Peter de Jonge*)

FAMILY OF PAGE-TURNERS

MIDDLE SCHOOL BOOKS

The Worst Years of My Life (*with Chris Tebbetts*) • Get Me Out of Here! (*with Chris Tebbetts*) • My Brother Is a Big, Fat Liar (*with Lisa Papademetriou*) • How I Survived Bullies, Broccoli, and Snake Hill (*with Chris Tebbetts*) • Ultimate Showdown (*with Julia Bergen*) • Save Rafe! (*with Chris Tebbetts*) • Just My Rotten Luck (*with Chris Tebbetts*) • Dog's Best Friend (*with Chris Tebbetts*)

I FUNNY SERIES

I Funny (*with Chris Grabenstein*) •
I Even Funnier (*with Chris Grabenstein*) •
I Totally Funniest (*with Chris Grabenstein*) •
I Funny TV (*with Chris Grabenstein*)

TREASURE HUNTERS SERIES

Treasure Hunters (*with Chris Grabenstein*) • Danger Down the Nile (*with Chris Grabenstein*) • Secret of the Forbidden City (*with Chris Grabenstein*) • Peril at the Top of the World (*with Chris Grabenstein*)

HOUSE OF ROBOTS SERIES

House of Robots (*with Chris Grabenstein*) •
Robots Go Wild! (*with Chris Grabenstein*)

OTHER ILLUSTRATED NOVELS

Kenny Wright: Superhero (*with Chris Tebbetts*) •
Homeroom Diaries (*with Lisa Papademetriou*) •
Jacky Ha-Ha (*with Chris Grabenstein*)

MAXIMUM RIDE SERIES

The Angel Experiment • School's Out Forever •
Saving the World and Other Extreme Sports •
The Final Warning • Max • Fang • Nevermore • Forever

WITCH & WIZARD SERIES

Witch & Wizard (*with Gabrielle Charbonnet*) •
The Gift (*with Ned Rust*) •
The Fire (*with Jill Dembowski*) •
The Kiss (*with Jill Dembowski*) •
The Lost (*with Emily Raymond*)

DANIEL X SERIES

The Dangerous Days of Daniel X (*with Michael Ledwidge*) •
Watch the Skies (*with Ned Rust*) •
Demons and Druids (*with Adam Sadler*) •
Game Over (*with Ned Rust*) •
Armageddon (*with Chris Grabenstein*) •
Lights Out (*with Chris Grabenstein*)

GRAPHIC NOVELS

Daniel X: Alien Hunter (*with Leopoldo Gout*) •
Maximum Ride: Manga Vols. 1–9 (*with NaRae Lee*)

For more information about James Patterson's novels, visit
www.jamespatterson.co.uk

Or become a fan on Facebook